Cernunnos Books
Hindi Tales of Mystery and Imagination
Volume 1

Dr. Archana VERMA (born 1946) obtained an MA with six gold medals from Allahabad University and she holds M.Litt. and Ph.D. degrees from Delhi University. She taught at the Department of Hindi, Miranda House, Delhi University from 1966 to 2011. She co-edited the Hindi literary magazine *Hans* with Rajendra Yadav from 1986 to 2008. Subsequently, she has been associated with the Hindi literary magazine *Kathadesh*, in which she has regularly authored an acclaimed column, 'Prasangvash' (By the Way) for five years. Dr Verma is the author of a young adult novel and two collections each of short stories, poems and literary criticism. She has edited the collected works of Rajendra Yadav (in fifteen volumes) and co-edited and co-directed a series of translations titled *Hashiye Ulanghti Aurat* (Women Crossing Boundaries).

A.K. KULSHRESHTH is the author of a short story collection and has translated two Hindi novels into English. His short stories have appeared in literary magazines and anthologies in eight countries.

HINDI TALES OF MYSTERY AND IMAGINATION

VOLUME I

Edited by
Archana Verma

Translated from Hindi
by A.K. Kulshreshth

Cernunnos
BOOKS

The short stories in this book were originally published in Hindi in
Kathadesh literary magazine,
Delhi, India in 2015

Hindi advisors: Dr Archana Verma and Dr Balwant Kaur
English literary editors: Dr Desiree Ward and N. Henaff

This translation © Cernunnos Books, 2015
Cover design by Zoya Chaudhary
Interior design by N. Henaff

ISBN: 978-981-11-2778-6

Contents

Hindi Tales

of Mystery and Imagination

Volume I

Stories of Mystery and Imagination in the Landscape of Hindi Fiction

Archana Verma

The Hindi story conducts itself with gravitas. This is not to say that there is no tradition of light literature, or that it is not being written today. As it happened with other Indian languages, the advent of the printing press in the late 19th century gave rise to a market for all kinds of Hindi works. This market germinated with the transfer of the stories of *kissa goi* – an oral storytelling tradition – on to printed paper. The ample stock of readily available material consisted of the genres of *tilasm aiyyari* (sorcery and fantasy), detective and ghost stories.

The production and consumption of this very saleable body of work has been going strong for about a hundred and fifty years, but our cultural values have bred distaste for its saleability in us. We have relegated this work to crumbling pavements, away from the high street. Literary fiction must not grip the reader; it must not be sensational or fast paced. Literature must be highbrow. Categories such as pop and pulp have been ignored by the literati, so that the majority of readers have distanced themselves from Hindi literature, which has become a medium of communication and debate for specialists. Pulp does not even have the second-hand respect that it has naturally obtained in the rest of the world, where it is acknowledged that in the world of art and literature, perception is often a function of packaging.

I had not thought about this until Cernunnos Books approached me and talked about their mission of fiction beyond borders, and their 'Hindi project' – their first project that aimed at popularising Hindi literature. They wanted our literary magazine *Kathadesh* to run the Hindi Tales of Mystery and Imagination Contest, the first contest of its kind. What they had in mind was not about packaging, though. They had put together a concept for participating writers, and this concept was about a 'serious' and interesting literature of mystery and imagination.

We announced the contest. Our writing community was excited about it, but we could sense they were also nonplussed. Mystery stories in *Kathadesh*? What were things coming to? We published Cernunnos's call for submissions multiple times in our print magazine, on our website (http://www.cernunnosbooks.com/projects.html), on Facebook. We explained that we had no intention of polluting Hindi literature or of lowering our collective standards for it – all we wanted to do was raise pop literature to a higher level. We extended the closing date, and reduced the threshold we had set for the minimum number of entries.

Most of the stories we received were stock stories of crime and suspense. They often had mystery as well. What we found mostly missing was imagination. In some cases, we found imagination that was too obviously forced. We chose seven stories instead of the ten that we had planned, because we wanted to be sure that the first of our volumes did justice to our objective.

So, here we have the seven translated stories from the first ever contest of its kind. When I read them together, I see that virtual reality – in some form or the other – is an element of the mystery in each story. The Indian bent of creativity has been fertilised with the concept of *maya* for centuries, and perhaps that makes it easy for writers to blur the lines between reality and virtual reality. This is just a thought that flashed in my mind, not a theory I have tested with research. I might be making a leap here.

This collection is a realisation of the Cernunnos team's imagination. It has created an atmosphere in

Hindi fiction. We don't know how long it will last, or how far it will go. You will decide that. As for me, I am happy that *Kathadesh* was its main platform and I, the editor.

Crazy for Peace

Premchand Gandhi

HIS IS WHERE THE CITY ENDS. There is a row of witnesses to that effect: a Muslim graveyard, a Christian cemetery, a Hindu cremation ground. After these last stops of the human journey, there is a deep valley. On the far side of the valley, there is dense jungle. Wolves and bats shriek from its depths at night. Oh, and the valley I mentioned is also a road of sorts. Trucks and tractors use it after gingerly descending its slopes.

Only a nut like me would go to a place like that to chill. I still highly recommend it if you have never seen graveyards and crematoria with locks on their main doors. The first time I was there, I thought the sites at the city's edge hadn't been inaugurated yet. Our politicians seem to all have a virus that requires them to plant stones with their names wherever they can, and I had not seen any signs of official sanction there. Anyway, the first day I could not see much, because dusk had descended before I drifted there. Later, I started going at the time of day when decent folks head homewards. That is where they find peace – they think. For me, the edge of the city worked better. The presence of the departed, the wolves, the evening song of other life forms – they all converged to lull me into a deep calm.

There was a well-constructed road there on which women, girls and boys learned to drive. Every evening, cars, motorbikes and scooters were put to the test. On the other side of the resting-place-complex, the young guys performed stunts on their modified motorbikes, to train for safaris and show how tough they were. I liked being part of that whole scene. No one knew me, of course. Or maybe they did know me as the weirdo who drove so far out of town with his windows rolled down to take in the air of that haunted corner of the earth. There was a spot I had staked out for myself. It was near the cemetery, under the shade of trees.

Once, I saw a tall, lithe woman practising on her scooter with her daughter riding pillion. Her fat husband was huffing away behind them. She had a confident smile.

'Okay, let's go', the husband panted.

'What's your problem?' The woman shouted, grinning. 'It's only the second day, and look, you don't even have to prop me up anymore!' She revved the scooter, a maroon Honda, and sped towards the main road outside the graveyard. The husband slumped and trudged along after her, shaking his head.

I thought about that woman – soon she would be able to drive to the children's school, to the market, to the movie theatre. The gearless scooter had unfettered a domesticated housewife. The next day, that woman could choose to drive around in her own neighbourhood. She didn't have to come to this safe trafficless corner any more. How many women were there like her? Millions, I hoped.

A blue Suzuki Zen rolled into view. The husband was teaching the wife. Their daughter held on to the left front seat and watched over her mother's shoulder with a frown of concentration. These people were exceptional. I had concluded from my studies that most men came here with their daughters. They probably delegated their wives' lessons to driving schools. A few women came alone in their cars.

There did not seem to be all that many young ones learning to drive two wheelers. It was probably because this generation had already learned cycling, and it was not such a big leap for them to ride motorbikes or scooters. So it was mostly housewives who came there.

One of those days, I was there, enjoying the clear lilting call of a cuckoo and trying to figure where it was coming from. It had this magical quality of filling the whole place. A woman stopped her scooter very close to me. Her elderly husband sat snuggled up to her, with his hands stretched out so that he held the handlebar from the outside.

'It's been years since I heard a cuckoo this way', she said. 'Let's stop for a while?' My eyes met the husband's. He did not say what was on his mind. He just kept up the gentle pressure on the accelerator. They were gone before the next call of the cuckoo rang out.

For many evenings, I drove straight to that spot and stayed there. One day, I decided to check out the grounds of the departed. I locked my car and walked to the first doorway. All the doors were locked, but when I circled around to the side that faced the valley, I saw that the locks were quite redundant. The walls were broken in many places. As I crossed the threshold of one of those gaping holes, I felt a pang of fear. What if there was someone inside? What would he think of me? I figured I would say I was looking for a drinking fountain. I pushed the thought away.

Inside, white grave stones formed an endless grid. Some of the graves had dry roses on them; others had the remnants of incense sticks and other accoutrements. A cool breeze came in from the jungle, caressed the graves and made its way towards the fumes of the city. There were two taps next to a borewell. In the open spaces, there were the shrunken remains of plants. As I walked along, I saw a couple of sheds in one corner. The walls of the sheds had inscriptions in Urdu, perhaps from the Koran –

because there were moral messages in Hindi as well that I could read. It struck me that it must have been ages since a funeral procession had landed up there. I couldn't see any new-looking grave. It gave me a sense of relief, in a perverse kind of way – the media had had a lot to say about the relationship between Muslims and death. There were signs that *diyas*, earthen lamps, had been lit in some places. Not a good idea, I said to myself. Lighting up that place seemed like celebrating death.

The evening sun was beating a retreat. The sounds of cars and scooters had faded away, and the birdsong was louder and deeper. I sensed that the wolves and bats would take over soon. When I headed back to the car, I saw a light shimmer in the valley. I peered, and made out a red car. I figured it must be someone boozing inside. I quickened my steps, and then froze. A long black snake slithered across the path, towards the valley. I soaked in the atmosphere for a few moments before I opened the car door. Soon, I became part of the din of the city.

You are probably a bit worried about me by now. It is not normal for a working guy to do what I used to do back then. You will probably have guessed that if I had a home, the chances were it had the stuff of homes. Internet, TV, music, the works. But in the unlikely event that you have imagined a wife and children, let me tell you they were not attached. I was alone then. I had been single for two months.

My parents had passed away a long time back. I had no brothers or sisters. There were a few relatives, and there was need-based contact with them. Their needs, not mine. I was not married, but was not a bachelor either. Until the break-up, I had lived with Nalini. We did not have a quarrel, or a child. I had met Nalini during a government project. She ran an NGO that worked to help abused women and also worked for women's health. I used her NGO for an official project. Nalini and I hit it off and ended up being happy together. On marriage, we agreed to do everything it entailed, without the ritual itself. And we were happy to be a DINK – double income no kids – couple on the verge of our forties. She was a *Mumbaiyya* – a Mumbai person – I, a local.

One day we split. I'll talk about it later. For now, seek peace, brothers and sisters.

The next time I wanted to check out the cemetery and the cremation ground. I suspected the experience wouldn't be too different from the Muslim graveyard, but that didn't matter. I had to travel for work, and a full week had passed before I drove towards the comfort of my favourite spot on the edge of the city.

It was the peak of summer. I picked up a bottle each of water and beer. I stopped the car at the usual place and sipped the beer. A woman dressed in a brown sari was practising driving on a scooter. Her plump boy sat behind her, enclosing her, with his hands on the handle. He was double her size, and I couldn't help writing off that lady's prospects of becoming a capable driver any time soon. I toyed with the idea of telling her she would be better off learning on her own. The two of them drove up and down that street twice, and in the end the boy drove the scooter away with the mother looking glum.

I remembered how we had learned to cycle. We would be peddling away, with the trainer – usually a family member – running behind us, steadying the cycle with one hand gripping the carrier at the back. One of those times, without our knowing it, they would let go. When we realised what had happened, not from the feel of the cycling but by looking over our shoulders, we would cry out in anger. The teacher would say they had to let go some time. On falling and getting cuts, they had this Brahma-like wisdom to offer: no one ever learned to cycle without getting a cut or two. Those were the days of the big black cycles – Hero, Atlas, Raleigh. Children's cycles were a luxury.

A car drove into the road between the graveyard and the cremation ground, and cruised to a halt. I had closed the doors for a change, because I was guzzling a beer. The windows were still open. I would take a swig when there was no one in sight. I saw two girls in the other car. They were about two hundred metres away. I guessed they were in their twenties. They lowered their windows and flicked off their seat belts. The driver gave me a cursory look-over, while the other girl lit up a long, thin cigarette with a match. She took a deep, long puff and handed it over to her friend, turning up the music at the same time. It was an English song. The strains reached me. I gulped some beer. I figured they had come here because they couldn't be seen smoking at home. I saw they were sipping from a 'mineral' water bottle in a way that meant either that they were following a health fad, or drinking vodka. A second cigarette followed the first one. I thought I might as well let them feel less inhibited. I finished the beer, and stepped out towards the cremation ground.

It was like the others I had seen. A row of sheds, below them the remnants of ashes drifting in the breeze. The smell of incense and ghee. A heap of coconut shells and incense packets. A haphazard timber yard in a corner, and a rusty balance dangling over a thick *neem* tree. The weights were an assorted bunch of stones. My fellow men had to make it a point to respect the local traditions of cutting corners until the very end. The attendant's number was emblazoned on the wall. The walls were otherwise sanctified by holy couplets, idioms and hymns. A small temple with broken doors housed a few idols covered by a layer of dust.

A few hundred steps away, the small cemetery was a fairly neat matrix of graves, all gathering dust like the idols in a temple. The graves had stones with the names of the deceased in Hindi and English. It was a little too simple, too austere. There were no sermons on the walls.

All the resting places had a few things in common. There were benches of cement gifted by relatives. The donors had their names firmly chiselled on to them. The names were visible through the sheath of dust that covered them. There were plenty of plants, but they had withered from neglect. Cleaning up had been left to the most eco-friendly of brooms, the wind.

The silence that you find in a place like that calms your soul, not just your brain. You feel a detachment. But I've always thought the detachment only lasts in that intersection of place and time. Maybe that's what drew me there again and again. I was happy with that spot I had found for my car, with the shade of the trees and the sights offered by the students of the art and science of driving.

What stopped me from descending into the valley and crossing it into the jungle? From feeling how it felt to walk on the riverbed? From studying the marks of the rainwater on the slops? The snake that had crossed my path – how many more were there like it? I thought of all that as I walked back to my car. And I reflected that if it wasn't for the Forest Department, a new town would have straddled the river by now.

As I walked along the edge of the valley, a rabbit scampered away and into the bush. I liked the sight. Some parts of the city had offered sightings of rabbits when I was a boy. Now, the only rabbits in the city were pets. I toyed with the idea of going down into the valley, but the sun was sinking and I knew its moments above the skyline would be short-lived. A tractor came into view on the riverbed.

We were filling the riverbed with the city's refuse, and scraping away its mud to make the city bigger. My sense of peace came undone. I strode back to the car. The two women had gone.

My house felt like a wasteland without Nalini. We

had decided to live in, to live together, Nalini and I. But the mindset that we have inherited makes the man feel like the husband, the protector and the mentor. We were quite clear-headed, and we had specifically agreed that we weren't the type to respect conventions. We would live the liberal life. We would trust each other; we would find our own pleasures with and without each other. Ah, the human mind – the male mind, it loves to shatter such fantasies. We broke up.

For weeks on end, I did not have time to go to my sanctuary. I chafed in the suffocating atmosphere at work. I had to do long tours of duty. The monsoon had started, and the media had begun to show images of the spruced up greenery of the city. It was a huge relief for me to head to the place at the end of the city one Sunday morning.

The trees looked victorious. Lush, vibrant foliage peered over the walls of the three resting places. I locked the car and headed down the valley.

It was breezy and cloudy. The air had the energising scent of monsoon and forest. I gulped it in, enjoying the press of my lungs against my ribs. The valley wasn't as steep as it looked. It was a bit of a mud road, with tracks of motorbikes, tractors and cars. So, cars could go as well… I dismissed the thought. I was better off on foot – I had fewer constraints of direction, and I could also imagine the car sinking slowly, but surely, into a sandy bed. There was a wild, natural garden on either side of the riverbed. I felt the sharp sting of an insect on my elbow. How many of those insects lived their brief lives during the monsoon? And did we know how much of our ecosystem depended on them? I swatted it hard, nevertheless.

The three years I had spent with Nalini had gushed by like the stream in front of me. The images of our times together played out in my mind. From the creator's perspective, was our life together like the lives of these insects? Birth, a life of some pleasure, perhaps, and a quiet death like the silent end of a day – was that what it was about?

The rainwater had cut up the riverbed into small gorges. As I walked on, I wondered how much of the forest was left intact up ahead. The streams that ran across the riverbed were streaked grey with the refuse of the city. This was how we repaid the river for the life force that it had given us. The tubewells that lined the path of the river were the city's main source of water. So, this was a form of recycling then. We took the river's water and fed it toxins. Parts of the riverbed were all slush, and the fragments of polythene trapped in the mud sang hymns to our great civilisation. As I walked on, the exhilarating freshness gave way to a stench. I made out a few animal carcasses in the distance. So, this was where the government performed their version of the last rites for dead animals. Just across from me now was the forest that had exerted such a pull on me, and still did, despite the stink.

My mind wandered to my most unpleasant day with Nalini. I had to go to Mumbai for work, and I had asked my personal assistant to book the flight. It happened so fast that I couldn't talk to Nalini about it. I dashed off home after lunch. We had our own sets of keys, so we didn't have a tradition of ringing the doorbell and all. That day, I went straight into my bedroom, changed and lay down in bed for a while. I always enjoyed those stolen moments of rest during a work day. On the threshold of sleep, I heard a door open.

'It was nice with you, Rohan. We'll meet again.' It was Nalini's voice, from her bedroom.

'It's been great, ma'am', a young man's high-pitched voice said. 'I'll never forget this.'

'No, you won't.' Nalini laughed. 'Don't worry, you know where to find me, right? Bye for now.'

'Bye ma'am.'

And the main door was opened and closed. A little later, Nalini's bedroom door was pulled shut. I was wide awake. I got my stuff together for the flight like a robot. While I was waiting for the flight, having completed the check in and security check, the time passed in a daze. It was only when I collapsed into one of the plastic seats in the waiting area that I noticed a pain in my chest. My fingers moved like an automaton's as I typed out a text message to Nalini. 'Enjoy your life with Rohan. I'm in Mumbai for a week.' Actually it was supposed to be three days. Anyway, I switched off the mobile.

I left the phone off in the evening when I got to Mumbai. When I switched it on again, there were dozens of missed calls from Nalini. And as many disjointed, frantic messages with explanations about Rohan's background, their relationship and other stuff. I suffered an overflow and my blurring eyes couldn't make sense of the messages. I deleted all of them. I texted her I couldn't stand the stink of lust at home, and that we should split. She didn't reply.

I moved on towards the jungle with my handkerchief tied over my nose. I found places where I could cross the tiny streams, and once I was on the far side I found a shady beaten path along *kikar* and *babool* trees. It was much better already, as if the smelly part of the valley had been screened off. The earth was still contaminated with sachets, plastic scraps and fragments of polythene, though. I tried to figure why the path had been made in the first place. Did people come here to graze animals? Was it the Forest Department chaps who trudged here? For now, there was no one around. A colony of industrious ants and a lot of chirpy birds were the only visible living beings around. At one point, I heard the swooshing sounds of an alarmed bird taking off, accompanied by the violent rustling of leaves. I figured I must have walked a kilometre by then.

I saw my first sign of real wildlife – a mongoose scurried across the clearing of the path. I remembered the snake I had encountered as I left the cemetery. Was the mongoose after a meal, perhaps the same snake, or was it running after a companion? The wild grass had flourished in the rains. I had watched the mongoose as it crossed the path. I wondered how many more animals must be slithering in the tall grass. I noticed that some of the trees had white arrows painted on them, and figured it must be work of the Forest Department staff. At one point, I was surprised to see a bold red 'X' marked on one of the trees, next to an arrow that pointed right. There were tyre tread marks in the wet mud there. Ahead of me, the forest seemed to become thicker and somehow more forbidding.

Nalini had kept trying to call me, although I did not take her calls. When I got tired of them, I texted her: 'I was at home that day when you and Rohan came out of your bedroom, okay?' She went silent after that.

I saw a smaller path climbing uphill to the right. I made my way towards it. It seemed to have been chopped out of the dense forest. As I walked on, the trees thinned out again. Up ahead of me, I saw a hillock that seemed to mark the start of the Aravali Mountains. I was sure there would be water on the other side – water that flowed from the mountains and fed the river. I knew it was one of those times, when the destination was further than it seemed to be, but something propelled me to keep going. The ground had become hard and rocky, and the forest had petered out. I left the footpath, and cut across to the hillock. A large movement at the corner of my left eye made me turn that way. It was a group of deers, not more than five hundred metres away. Their movements were fluid and effortless. I wished I could slow time down to savour the moment. I looked at my watch. I had been walking for two hours, so I must have done something like eight kilometres.

Wasn't it a bit like my time with Nalini? I had kept plodding on, then something happened that I could never have imagined. Was this how it was meant to be? Did we have to journey through life, so that it would take us deep into its folds and then reveal to us secrets without which we could understand neither ourselves nor others?

When I got to the hillock, I saw a line of stones neatly laid out on a flat area, as if someone had made seating arrangements. As I stepped forward, I sensed that I would see a rainwater lake. I stepped on to a small plateau that was just wide enough for two normal single beds. My legs told me I had walked enough. I sat down there, and watched the reflection of the cloudy sky in the water. A flock of birds was making merry at the edge of the lake. I had never seen so much clean water in recent memory. I lay down and enjoyed the feeling of the cold hard ground on my back. I wanted to stay for a long time, watching the clouds float by.

A place like that can make you feel all primitive and romantic. I shouted out my own name. 'Sanjay!' The birds cried back to me. When I got up after a while, I saw that in the distance the surface of the lake had become frosted. It was drizzling there, and the rain front was somewhere between the lake and where I sat. I was dry. I got up and walked around. I noticed things in the bushes – wrappers of food, bottles of beer and drink, shreds of torn cloth. I couldn't help analysing the trash. The cloth fragments were pieces of handkerchiefs, and *chunnis*, neck scarves. There were pieces of bangles, and used condoms. I looked another time at the paradise that wasn't all that far from this vicious trash. I wanted to go back. I walked away from the hillock. I had just started out when I saw a flurry of movement in the valley, far away. It was a pack of wolves come to one of their watering holes. My breath quickened and my heart pounded with fear, although they were far and I was much higher than them. I looked back and wondered at all that trash again.

Who the hell would have used this place as a love nest? A bunch of young ones must have discovered it the way I did, and then anointed it as the place for love-making. I thought about Nalini. The idea of the two of us in a place like this was stupid – she loved comfort and she had never shared my love of adventure and the outdoors. Still, the idea of sex in the forest turned me on.

I walked much faster on the way out of the forest, descended into the valley, and shortly after, sank into the comfort of my car. I leant back and lazed for some time. I had parked off the road this time, near the usual spot. The car wasn't visible unless you looked hard for it.

In the rear-view mirror, I saw a guy on a motorbike, and a tall, svelte woman in a maroon sari on a scooter. When he took off his helmet, I saw that the guy had the kind of rugged look that attracts women. They smiled knowing smiles at each other. The breeze blew fragments of their conversation to me.

'… fun in the sun?'

'No, *yaar*, it's fun but it's scary. That wolf last time…'

'… stray dog.'

'No way, not that deep in the forest.'

'Well … evening … daylight now.'

'It will be evening by the time…'

'… quick one.'

'Last time … the chunni, my mother-in-law…'

'… sari today…'

'… starts bawling…'

'Get on the bike… faster.'

'This?'

'…'

'I'm scared, honestly.'

The guy flashed a smile, snapped his fingers and drove towards the cemetery. The woman followed him.

I called Nalini that evening. Her phone rang for a long time. I was setting a limit on how many times I would redial when she took the call.

'So, what was all that about independent lives?' She was controlled and I imagined her face tight with anger. She was the type to use menace more than theatrics.

'Independence is fine. I never meant, like completely open. If you were in my place, I can just about imagine the ruckus you would have created. "Government officer frolics with girlfriend in common-law spouse's presence!" Or maybe something tighter, the copy editor would do a better job. But you know what I mean. And the women's organisations would have been on your side, ready to shred me. And I, who would I have to turn to?'

I heard a sigh and I imagined her rolling her eyes. 'You retard, no one's a spouse here. And you're so many miles off the mark… We had a relationship of consent, right?'

I got the feeling that I was the one being uptight, and that infuriated me.

'Okay, then there's no more consent. We're both free.'

'What does that mean?'

'We're splitting. I'll stay out another day, and I suggest you move back into your old place when I return.'

'Okay. Is that all you have to say?' She was choking.

'No. Take care, and I hope you do well in life.' I had become hoarse, and I hated it. She started crying, and I cut the call.

My thoughts wandered to that couple who had ridden down the valley on a motorbike towards the jungle. I saw them go down the slope. They did not wear helmets. The motorbike was zipping at a speed that made me dizzy. Ah, the fearlessness of youth.

The woman was clinging tight to the guy. I had walked over closer to the edge. I could still make them out in the distance, heading for the forest. I did not know why, but I went into the cemetery. I found the scooter tucked away between a pair of trees. I sat on it and rocked back and forth. It struck me that she was the woman I had seen many days before, the one who was learning to drive and whose husband had huffed after her. It must have been a month or so since then. Yes, it was her all right. Her husband was dark and shorter than her.

I felt sorry for him – and for myself. I had come here in search of peace. Even if it was a freakish thing to do, I had not expected to find myself in this tawdry cesspool. I saw that they had left their helmets hanging on the handle, and the key in the ignition. They must really have been taken by a fit of passion. I pulled out the key and opened the storage compartment with it, even as I cursed myself for my prurience. There was a pair of gloves, a scarf to tie around the mouth and a pack of visiting cards. I picked one up. It read, 'Kamakhya Saris' in brilliant red, and gave a Guwahati address. So, the husband had a business in Guwahati, and she stayed here in town. Well, love is the best source of solace, if that's what you're looking for. I clicked the compartment shut, put the key back in the ignition and walked towards my car.

As I drove away, I said a respectful goodbye to the three resting places. You could find peace here all right, but the chances were higher if you were dead.

In the real world, your best bet – if you wanted peace – was to find a soulmate who could help you grapple with each day.

The next day, I had given up that forlorn edge of the city.

The day after, the newspaper headlines screamed that a pack of wolves had shredded a pair of lovers to death on the outskirts of the city. The woman's name had been kept secret, but the man's name was Rohan. The next day, the obituaries featured an announcement of a *tiya*, a ceremony performed on the third day after death. It had a mournful picture of the svelte woman. Her name was Kanchan, and her folks and her husband's side had organised two separate prayer meetings for her. Another corner of the same page announced a prayer meeting for Rohan. His father was a retired Superintendent of Police. The guy in the picture was very much the fun-loving bike rider. I tried to correlate him with the Rohan who had changed my life. Their voices had nothing in common. The dead guy had a much deeper, gruffer voice. Did Rohan have more than one persona? Or were there many ladykiller Rohans?

Kanchan was probably cremated in the ground near the place she had learned driving. I couldn't help thinking of her cuckolded husband, who must have come in a hurry from Guwahati to perform her last rites. Was he sorry he had taught her to drive? Or was he thinking that a wife like that had got what she deserved? Was he at peace now?

I was flicking through emails in office on a hot afternoon. An email from Nalini popped up. The subject was 'Some facts about Rohan'. Trust her to write it like a memo. I minimised the mailbox and got back to the manual notation that I had to make on the paper files that carried the flow of the government's work. The email had distracted me, and I couldn't help thinking of Rohan and Kanchan.

Were they done, sated and happy in each other's arms when the wolves got to them? Or were they still making love when it happened? There was only one way out of there – the path I had taken. The only other way out was a sheer drop from the plateau. If only they had finished and been on the motorbike, they might have escaped alive. The press reports said that the first witnesses, the Forest Department workers, found little remaining of the ravaged lovers. The wolves must have been ferocious, and the birds had been at them later. What a horrible way to go. The motorbike was parked on one side, and their mobile phones had made identification easy.

When the office emptied out, I read Nalini's email. I left the office in a thoughtful mood. As I drove out of the parking area, I saw Nalini standing on the left.

I stopped and opened the door, and she climbed into my car without a word.

'Where's your car?' I asked.

'I took a taxi', she said. 'The car's at home.'

'Whose home?'

'Our home, retard', she said and smiled. I was laughing before I knew it, and she joined me, laughing together.

'And I thought Rohan … the wolves?'

She fished out a folded newspaper from her bottomless bag, after searching for a rather long time. 'Here – this one is about the wolf-attack-Rohan. He's not the Rohan I know.'

I slowed the car to a halt on the side of the road. The headline read, 'Spoilt son was headed for a disastrous end.' The four-column story below told of Rohan's nasty, short and brutal life. It seemed he had faced charges of theft, arson and molestation multiple times, but his father's influence saw him go free each time. Anonymous neighbours had said that they would not be grieving for him.

'Hmm … so, this Rohan was a bit of a wolf himself. And your Rohan…'

'He's a transgender. I also work for them, okay?' she said. She unfolded and refolded the paper so that it showed another story. 'Transgender refuses to marry, bucks family pressure.' A transgender from the posh Civil Lines area of town had filed a complaint against his family. He had charged them with pressuring him to marry a woman so that they did not lose face. The police had counselled the family, and the charge was withdrawn. 'All I want to do is lead a normal life', the story quoted the victim as saying. It said the victim had an MBA and worked for an MNC.

'Are you gonna spend all evening here?' she said.

I felt a sharp pinch on my shoulder.

I thought of something to say, but the words didn't quite form. I gulped and turned the ignition on.

Vasco Da Gama Street

Pratibhu Bannerjee

THEY SAY THERE ARE MOMENTS when something said in fun becomes a prophecy. It must have been one of those moments when Anubha quipped about Shekhar's infidelity. Why else would Polomi have come into his life?

She was in the crowd outside the exit gate at Guwahati airport. Shekhar felt warmer at the very sight of her. She looked beautiful in a stylish black-red batik kurta and a pair of jeans. He waved to her, and she waved back, her open palms tracing wide arcs. He manoeuvred his trolley towards the gap in the railing that served as a partition for the passenger area. He was grinning and could not take his eyes off her. He felt a dull thud in his right shoulder blade as a stocky man collided into him and moved on. Shekhar almost fell on his face. He steadied himself in a few faltering steps, and opened his mouth to shout, but he was too stunned to speak when the man looked over his left shoulder. The cold, murderous look had a familiarity to it. That plump guy, average in height, with his thick neck and clenched jaws – this was their third or fourth encounter. Each time, Shekhar got the feeling that he was trying to make his presence known. And a little more than that. The man wanted to intimidate Shekhar, and he was succeeding.

Two days ago, Shekhar was walking to his hotel, down Hillcourt Road in Siliguri, after finishing a day's work. A car lurched close to him and sped away. His heart had pounded. The car slowed down after a few hundred metres and did a U-turn, now moving at a slow and steady speed. It slowed to a crawl on the opposite side of the road, and the dark frosted window glass slid down. It was the same man, with the same malevolent stare. Shekhar was too stunned to react. And it was that same man who had singed Shekhar's hand with a cigarette in a very theatrical way on Park Street in Kolkata. He had burned his hand and started to walk away, making a point to turn back to give him that malevolent look. There was something menacing about the man that made Shekhar shrink back. The burning on his hand gave him heartburn when he thought about it later. He cursed himself for not striking back.

And here he was again.

So, who was this man, and why was he shadowing Shekhar? Shekhar's forehead was creased when he got out of the crowded exit area. His friends had warned him about the trouble with the extremist ULFA – United Liberation Front of Assam – when he had started work in Guwahati. Did it have something to do with those guys? Or was it something else?

The sunlight had mellowed when his budget flight took off from Siliguri to Guwahati. Siliguri is the hub in North Bengal that connects the North-East of India to the rest of the country. In a few minutes, the magnificent snowy Himalayas appeared on his left.

With the other passengers, Shekhar feasted his eyes on the golden mountains. He settled back in his seat and enjoyed a relaxed feeling that he had not had in several days of work. Being a steel trader meant that work took him from Raipur to Kolkata, Siliguri to Guwahati for days on end. And to complete the flow of material, he also went to the Badbil area of Orissa, from where illegally mined iron ore was fed to private steel plants of all sizes in his hometown, Raipur. There was money in the trade, but the workload was a killer. When he had entered the trade, the biggest *mandi*, market, for steel was in Govindpur, in Punjab. In just over ten years, Raipur had displaced it, and Shekhar had moved from Ludhiana, near Govindpur, to Raipur. It was his business that had brought him on this trip.

'Don't you find air travel boring?' Anubha had teased him when he was preparing for the trip. 'It doesn't have the charm of train journeys, no? You save time, but you don't have the hawkers, and the passengers aren't as friendly. I just don't like flights.'

'I don't understand your complex about flying', Shekhar had said, a little peeved, even as he continued packing. 'You never forget to tell me about it.'

'Why would I? The boring security checks, painted ground staff and air hostesses with their fake smiles, and their even more fake Hindi accents – those accents really hurt my ears, by the way. And that unclear and dreary announcement from the cockpit. It's as if flying the plane exhausts the pilots so much that they can't even talk properly.' Shekhar knew that Anubha was enjoying teasing him, and that she could tell it was working.

'On the other hand, there's a catwalk of sexy women inside the plane', he said. He got back his poise and joined her game.

'Oh yah, right', Anubha smiled. 'Catwalk, sexy women, I'm sure that's a perk of air travel, especially for you. You are a man, after all, and men prefer the delicacies of others more than what's on their own plates.'

'Is that right?'

'You bet! You men, you will fill your plates, but then try to eat from someone else's plate.'

When he stepped out of Guwahati airport, Shekhar found himself thinking about that exchange with Anubha. The thing was, he realised with a pang when he saw Polomi up close, she was right.

Polomi hugged him and spoke into his ear. 'Hi Shekhar, you took so long this time.' He enjoyed the touch of her body.

'Yes, it's been too long', he said. 'You're looking beautiful.' He smelled her perfume. The strange man and Anubha disappeared from his mind's eye – at least for a moment.

'I have to think up a new lie every time I come', Polomi said. 'This time I said I had work at the Bihu Dance Academy.' She snuggled up to him in the back seat, ignoring the taxi driver. Shekhar squeezed her thigh and smiled back at her.

The road to the city centre is often jammed in the evening. The taxi had to stop many times before they reached Paan Bazaar. The darkness had thickened by the time they reached the hotel.

'What's the matter?' Polomi said. They were in their hotel room. 'You look worried.'

'No, not really. When I'm with you, I feel other things. There's no room for worry. You look beautiful. Honestly, you look better each time I see you.' He pulled Polomi to him and on to the bed.

But Polomi was right. He was tense. He just didn't want to tell Polomi about the man. The thing was, he had seen him in the traffic jam. This man had become like a spectre to Shekhar. Who the hell was he? What did he want?

Shekhar had a day's work in Guwahati, but he had planned to stay for three days to spend time with Polomi. He had been doing this for a year now. But this time, it seemed the spectre would haunt him and spoil his stay.

The next day, they went to Kaamakhya Maa temple. The temple was on a hill in the middle of Guwahati City. As usual, there was a long line, and it took a long time for them to reach the inner sanctum. In the dim light, amidst the throng, Shekhar found solace as they prayed before the Goddess, the source of creative feminine energy. Shekhar felt much better when they came out of the temple. Polomi was looking at him with wide, shocked eyes.

'What happened to your clothes? They were fine when we stepped in!' She said.

Shekhar looked at them. They were stained with blood and bird feathers. He had thought it was sweat.

'They look like pigeon feathers', Polomi said. 'How did this happen inside the temple? It's probably sacrificial blood.'

He felt numbed.

'Look, it couldn't have happened inside', Polomi continued. 'It's true there are sacrifices – goats and pigeons – but they are done outside, and blood is forbidden in the inner sanctum.'

Shekhar's mind reeled. Where did all this blood come from? He thought of the man who had been hounding him. He returned from the temple feeling oppressed and jumpy. What next? Where would the spectre strike? But the rest of the day passed without another incident. The man did not appear at the hotel, or in the bazaar.

It was his last night with Polomi.

'What's up? You look happy.' Polomi sounded upset. 'Why? Because you'll be free of me and back in the arms of your wife?' She had spent the day with him, and as soon as they had returned to the room she changed and lay next to him. She looked delicious in a transparent nightdress, but she had seemed somewhat uneasy that evening.

'Don't be silly', Shekhar said. 'Our friendship doesn't have anything to do with my married life. You know how special you are to me.' He pulled her closer. The curves of her splendid young body, clearly visible through the flimsy nightdress, had worked their unfailing magic on him.

Polomi pushed his hand away and sat up.

'What's up?' He asked.

'I have something to say', she said. She took his hand in hers.

Shekhar sat up as well. In their year-old relationship, Polomi had always given him a pleasant sendoff. She had never been this moody.

'Be careful', she said, suddenly, with her chest heaving. She held him tight. Her breath was shallow on his cheek.

'What– Why?' Shekhar felt his heart thudding.

She did not say a word. Now this was scary.

'Say something. What are you worried about?'

She just sat there, eyes lowered, silent. The room felt oppressive. After a while, she got off the bed, picked up the bottle of 'mineral water', guzzled it down and came back to sit next to him.

He could make out that she was trying hard to control herself. Her breaths were artificially controlled and deep.

'You know ULFA has announced a strike tomorrow, right?' she said. 'You'll be better off if you leave for the airport before daybreak. No taxi-driver will take the risk of driving you there in broad daylight. I won't be able to come with you either.' She looked passive as she stroked his hair.

'But what will I do sitting in the airport all day?' Shekhar's flight was at three. He was uneasy. He had this sense that there was something Polomi wasn't saying.

'Sweetheart, you'll sit there and think of me, what else?' Polomi smiled. 'Ah, I'll just go crazy.'

Polomi's smile vanished. 'You're not the only one who'll be inconvenienced by the strike. People in Assam have been living with these strikes for thirty-five years. ULFA can call a strike any time. In the early years, they had a lot of public support. They used to talk about Assamese identity and autonomy. But later they started talking separation. And when they took to arms, you know the rest. Life here has been troubled since then.'

Shekhar was relieved to find firm ground for a discussion.

'You know', he said, 'when I made up my mind to start work here two years ago, people had warned me about the ULFA. I had been hearing about them, their separatist movement, their violence, and the ban on them. But I didn't know that they extorted money from outsiders who come here to do business.' Shekhar thought of the spectre, and a shiver ran through him.

A frightful thought crossed his mind. What if the ULFA had him in their sights? And if they had, why had they not yet talked directly about money? Were they softening him up first? Or was it something else? A rival out to get him? Would he even make it home safely this time? And why had Polomi warned him? Did she know something more than she was letting on? Or was his relationship with Polomi a problem for someone else?

'Why are you so worried?' Polomi asked. 'It'll be okay. I'm there for you. You'll only be bored a few hours at the airport, dear. And you're much into reading. Just read something – it won't be a problem.' She rested her head on his chest.

Communicating with women always helps men release their tension, Shekhar thought as he embraced Polomi. She wrapped herself around him with a fervour that pleased him.

The doorbell rang.

'Who can it be?' Shekhar was suddenly frantic with fear.

Polomi got up with a start and went to into the bathroom. She could not be seen in that nightdress, of course, with her womanhood bursting out of it.

One of the hotel staff stood at the door. Shekhar raised an eyebrow.

'Sorry, sir, a gentleman just left this for you', the man said, handing an envelope to Shekhar. 'He said it was urgent, so I had to come right away.'

'All right, thanks', Shekhar said, and flashed a smile as a formality as he shut the door.

'Who was it?' Polomi asked.

'Hotel staff. Asking when we'll check out', Shekhar lied. He tucked the envelope into his bag.

'Of all the times he could have chosen', Polomi said. She stretched lazily on the bed. She looked hungry and inviting, and she knew it. Shekhar went to her.

But he found her company did not give him respite from his worries. He could not help wondering about what accident would come up next. And accidents didn't come with warnings.

He fished out the envelope as soon as he had a seat to himself at the airport. He had been tempted to look during the taxi ride, but had controlled himself. Who knew, the driver could be in with the strange man.

It was an ordinary khaki coloured envelope. Inside was a pinkish page that looked like it was torn out of a writing pad, the kind that stationery shops usually stock. He looked at it for a long time. It struck him that his fingers were trembling. The page was blank, except for a large 'X' drawn across it.

What did it mean? Who would send a letter like that, and why? First, a stranger had hounded him in Kolkata, Siliguri and here in Guwahati, and then there was the bloody incident in the temple. And now, this. What was going on? His mind reeled. Was the ULFA after him? Or was it the Naxalites, again? Those guys were at it in Chhatisgarh, the state that his town Raipur was capital of. Wait a minute – what if Anubha found out now about Polomi, and she was the one behind all this? Or was it something else altogether?

He felt a pang of guilt. Even if Anubha had found out, she wasn't capable of this. What if someone else was after Polomi?

He looked around. There were the usual passengers, airline staff and security men in fatigues. No one looked suspicious. No one was looking at him.

He sat there and tried to control his ragged breath. He thought of Anubha and Gudiya. Gudiya, his daughter, whom he had left sleeping in her faded pink frock. Would he reach their welcoming arms safe and sound?

He picked up Paulo Coelho's *The Zahir*, his favourite, from the bag. Reading it gave him solace. He got the feeling that there was no danger to him then and there. The exaggerated security measures in the airport, the armed soldiers with their tense, anxious eyes, gave him a sense of safety.

When the flight from Kolkata touched down at Raipur, Shekhar felt a calm descend on him. The uneventful return journey, the sense of almost being home, comforted him. There was nothing to fear.

Sahdev stood waiting outside. He reached for the trolley with his familiar, deferential manner. Shekhar felt like reaching out and hugging him. For the first time, he felt that Sahdev wasn't just another employee. They walked quietly to the car, a grey Indigo. Sahdev placed his suitcase in the boot, held a door open for Shekhar, got into the driver's seat, and turned on the ignition and the air conditioning in practised, smooth moves.

'How's it going, Sahdev? Is everything okay?' he asked as he flung the bag to one side and sank into the rear seat. He felt strong and confident as he spoke. Actually there was no need to ask. His staff kept him updated on office matters anyway, on his mobile.

'Yes, *Bhaiyya.*' Sahdev always addressed Shekhar as *bhaiyya*, elder brother. 'All is well', Sahdev said with a smile.

In the last half-century, the poorest people from the poor Khariyar Road-Kantabanji belt of Western Orissa had gravitated towards Raipur. Down the years, they drove rickshaws, sweated in shops and hospitals, and worked as domestic servants. They had now become an integral part of Raipur society. The fringe areas of town that they settled in became the inner neighbourhoods of the vastly expanded city. Like the course jute lining on a fine silk cloth, their slums were a part of the fabric of the posh colonies of town.

Sahdev was one of the many such migrants who had never known another hometown. He had been with Shekhar for five years. He lived in Jagannath Para, one of the slums that coexisted with Shekhar's wealthy neighbourhood of Shankar Nagar. Sahdev was his driver and personal secretary.

Shekhar took in the comforting sights of town as the car navigated the traffic. How the city had changed in a few years. It was bursting at the seams, turning into a metro.

But at what cost? Whether it was Delhi, Bangalore, Guwahati or Pune, or the smaller hill towns like Ranchi, Rourkela or even Bhilai – all of them had sacrificed their green landscapes to this beast called development. Now it was Raipur in the teeth of the beast. Ancient trees were hacked down with a callousness that even surpassed that of the other cities.

Shekhar liked to stop by at the office on his way home. Sahdev took VIP Road and the highway that intersected the city. At Telibandha, he asked:

'*Bhaiyya*, you'll go to your office first, right?'

It took a while for Shekhar to register the question.

'No', he said. 'Drive home. I don't feel like going to the office.'

Shekhar sensed Sahdev stiffening with surprise, even as he turned the car deftly.

Anubha brought him a glass of water in a tray, as usual. He gently pushed it aside, and crushed her in his arms. She hugged him back, clumsily, still holding the tray with one hand. There was something about his embrace that had been missing for a long time now. Maybe it was the different, fervent beat of his heart? For years, Shekhar had driven straight to work from the airport or railway station. She had got used to it.

'Let go, you'll spill the water', she said. She was still tingling all over, and her voice was husky.

Shekhar crushed her even harder. It was such a relief to be back home in one piece. He could not explain it to her, of course.

'Gudiya will be back any time, and the ayah is with her', Anubha said in a whisper. She didn't know what had made Shekhar change, and she didn't care. She basked in his warmth.

Shekhar held on tight for some more time, and then relaxed his grip. He looked into her clear brown eyes. 'Is everything okay?'

'Yes, *Baba*, all okay. Go freshen up, I'll get breakfast.' She handed him the glass of water and gave him a smile that made her look even lovelier. 'Oh, will you go to office today?' she asked as if she had just remembered something.

'No, *yaar*, I don't feel like it. Let's go out when Gudiya is here – just the three of us.'

She smiled again, and he followed the comforting contours of her body as she walked away.

Shekhar took a shower and they sat down to breakfast. It was soothing to talk about the facts of everyday life – Gudiya, her school, the neighbours, a few relatives who mattered.

'Oh, I forgot to tell you on the phone – a man came with a letter for you, the day before yesterday.'

'What man?' Shekhar tensed.

'I hadn't seen him before.'

'What did he look like? Where's the letter?'

'Hmm, he was fat, short... He looked like he was from the North-East.'

'Where's the letter? Didn't you read it?'

'I'll get it *Baba*, I haven't made a veggie of it, no?' She tilted her head at him as she smiled and got up.

Shekhar could feel his heart thudding against his ribs. Anubha tore the envelope at one side, pulled out a pink sheet of paper and gaped at him.

'It's... blank', she said. 'Look, just a big cross on a blank paper.'

Shekhar kept his breath steady with an effort. He took the letter. His fingers were clammy. The envelope was the same khaki colour, and the page inside was the same pink as the one he had got in Guwahati.

'What's going on? You look pale all of a sudden', Anubha said. He saw her forehead was lined with worry.

'It's nothing', Shekhar said. 'I just remembered... I'll have to go to office, after all.' He knew he wasn't convincing. He couldn't keep the feverish thoughts from pummelling him. Could it be that the ULFA guys had their men among the Naxalites of this part of the country? Or ... could it be Anubha staging all this to stop his philandering?

'You're acting strange', Anubha said. He saw her lips had formed that angry pout of hers. 'First you say you're taking us out, and then you say you have to work. You think you can do whatever you like. That's not happening, not today. If you're tired after the journey, stay put at home, okay?'

'Let me go, please', Shekhar said. 'I'll see Dr Gupta… I actually didn't feel like going to work at all. It's just … very important. I'll only make a quick stop at the office on my way back from the doctor's.' Shekhar cringed as he heard himself sound phoney-meek. If only he could tell her all about it, and take her advice, he would be able to get that oppressive load off his mind. And what a burden it was, to suspect her of so much evil, and know that he was crazy to think that way, and still want to take shelter in her strength. If only he could tell her that he needed to be on his own to figure out this web of intrigue he had landed into. And there was no place better than his office chamber when he needed to be on his own.

He went straight into his chamber and sank into his pushback chair with his eyes closed. He had only stopped to tell the office boy to get him a coffee. Should he start off by talking to Polomi? She had been tense on their last night together, and had asked him to be careful. What was that about? She had said everything would be all right. What was it that she had expected to set right? Did she know what the danger was, and who it was from?

He called her mobile. The ring went on, but she didn't take the call. Was she busy? Or was she sulking because he hadn't yet found time to call her since leaving her? His thumb moved involuntarily to redial. This time, the call got cut after the first ring. Not good. Polomi had never done that. He couldn't help calling her again. He held the mobile tight against his ear, only to hear an out-of-reach message. He got up and paced the room. In the next few minutes he lost track of the number of times he tried her. He got the same irritating message each time.

He had come to the office with a plan of action only to be stuck at the first step. What now? He felt exhausted. He collapsed back into his chair and sat huddled for a long time. A phone call and an icy, crisp reminder from Anubha propelled him back home. In the car, he sat with his head hung back, drained of all energy.

The walk from the car to his bed seemed too much for him. He saw a blurred image of Anubha, tight-lipped but worried, before he crashed into a deep, aching sleep. He sensed Anubha by his side, with her back against the head of the bed, her troubled eyes on him.

He woke up before dawn. Gudiya was sleeping next to him, with her thumb in her mouth. Anubha had slept sitting, propped up by a pillow in her nightdress.

He had troubled her so much, Shekhar realised. It was clear she had no clue what was going on. If she did, she wouldn't have behaved this way. She would probably have kicked up a storm.

Shekhar's eyes strayed to his mobile. He picked it up and unlocked the screen. As his vision cleared slowly, he saw there was an email from Polomi. He sat up with a start. The email was sent around midnight. He had never imagined she would take such a risk. He looked again at Anubha and Gudiya, and took comfort from the steadiness of their breaths. He crept out of the bedroom, navigating its familiar geography carefully, and in the dining room he devoured the message. It was a long one.

'Sweetheart, this time you didn't even remember me after you left. I had thought I wouldn't talk to you when you called. Then, when you grovelled, I would forgive you. After what happened to me in the last few hours, you will never be able to flatter my anger away. We will never talk again. I won't use this number ever. I don't know if you will remember me. I will always carry sweet memories of our time together.

'All my life, I have longed for the kind of pleasure you gave me in our time together. I didn't tell you that I am married, because I didn't want to end that pleasure. Kishan Gogoi, the man who has tormented you, is my husband. We've just been married two years, and we kind of split eight months into the marriage, because of the way he treated me. I never got a husband's love and care. I only got unbearable mental and physical cruelty. Ever since I walked out on him, he has been after me to move back. When you came into my life, I was broken and alone. You made my life worth living. As you will have guessed, my husband found out about us, and he can't bear it. He saw us together when you were here before this last trip. He followed us to the hotel and got your Raipur address from the hotel reception. He went to Raipur – to your house and your office. I've just learned about all this. He was with me when you called. He cut your second call and then pulled out the battery.

'You are not his target, but he wants to show you and me that he can harm you. He knows I can't bear even the thought. There's someone close to you who is Kishan's informant. Kishan knew your whole itinerary this time. He used it to harass you systematically. You were in trouble, but you chose not to tell me about it.

'I saw him on your last evening here. I felt very afraid – I know what he's capable of. I've decided that it's best to keep you out of harm's way. I will move back with him. I'm writing this to you as he's gone off to get drunk – to celebrate his victory over me. He told me everything in the flush of his win, but he didn't say who his informant is. He let out that whoever it is lives on Vasco Da Gama Street, but then he pulled himself together. Be careful, you still have an enemy near you, someone who works for him. You will stay on in my heart.'

Shekhar's head throbbed. He called Polomi without thinking. Her phone was dead.

So, Polomi had left his life. She had sacrificed herself for him – what horrors would befall her? How had she felt when she made the decision to go back to her husband? Did she just see it as some kind of repayment of a debt, for the happiness she had got from their time together? Or was this love? A love that she had not overtly declared, even today. He had known Polomi, but why had he never understood her?

He looked out of an open window. It was dark outside – inky black like the blackness of his heart, that only he knew about. Not Polomi, not Anubha. He sighed and deleted the email. He trudged back to bed and basked in the warmth of his wife and daughter.

Morning came, and light filtered through his tired eyes. Shekhar woke early, and sat slumped in bed for a long time.

'Be careful', Polomi had said, and the words echoed in his mind. The threat had not yet passed.

Yes, he would be careful. Thanks to Polomi, he was not fighting blindfolded any more. He knew the origin of the attacks he had to fend off. Vasco Da Gama Street. He had never heard of it in his ten years in Raipur. He had passed pretty much every corner of the city by now. But he must find the street and figure who it was who lived there.

Who could tell him about it?

Suresh was the man, he decided. He was a real estate agent, and a native of the city. It was his business to know every inch of the city. Would he be up? Before he knew it, Shekhar had called the number.

'Hmm. Vasco Da Gama Street? Yaar, in all these years, I've never heard the name…' Suresh's slurred voice trailed off. Suresh was one of those sleep lovers who could only appreciate the beauty of a sunrise when they had stayed up all night. Shekhar had woken him up, knowing fully well that it would not be a welcome interruption. It turned out to be useless as well.

Who else could he turn to? He couldn't just sit around, waiting for the next attack.

It would be some time before Sahdev reported for duty. Shekhar went through the morning routine in a blur. He knew he was hurting Anubha again, but he couldn't stop himself from rushing out without waiting for the breakfast she was cooking up. He drove straight to Jayastambh Chowk, took the exit that went to Golbazaar, and parked near the main Post Office. Who would know the back alleys of the city better than the postmen? And here there were dozens of postmen. One of them must know Vasco Da Gama Street. He whistled to himself as he went in. It wasn't crowded yet.

No luck. Shekhar sat slumped in the car for a while before he turned it on. So, he had not heard of Vasco da Gama Street in his ten years living in the city, Suresh – who was born and bred in the city – had not heard of it … and now, it turned out that the postmen had not either.

Shekhar spent the next two days dredging the city. He skipped meals, missed work deadlines, endured verbal lashings from Anubha and sulks from Gudiya. It was no good.

Shekhar sat doodling at his desk, looking at a crude map of the city and the notes he had scribbled on his pad. His cheap blue-and-white plastic pen now traced a meaningless path across the paper. Was there really a Vasco Da Gama Street? Was the spy an employee? A friend? A fellow trader? He chided himself for the thought, but it kept coming back – it could be someone he trusted. Anubha, Sahdev, Suresh. He hated himself for this descent into cynicism. He could have bounced ideas of Polomi, but she was out of reach. Or was it a plot to torture him mentally? Maybe there was no Vasco Da Gama Street?

On the fourth day of his quest for Vasco da Gama Street, Shekhar sat deep in his armchair, leaning back until he could see the ceiling. The day before, he had made a list of all the people he could open his heart to, and ask for help. For different reasons, he had struck off the names one by one. Now, after a long day out in the sun, he sat back and thought about the things that had happened to him. He realised he had ignored a knock at his open door.

He straightened up. It was Sahdev. He placed a brown envelope on the table and said:

'*Bhaiyya*, someone gave this letter to Samharu.'

Old Samharu had worked as a guard for as far back as anyone could remember. He had grown frail, but he was reliable and hard-working. Shekhar kept a straight face with an effort. He just nodded. As soon as Sahdev turned his back, Shekhar shut the door, picked up the envelope and ripped the side open. He took a deep breath to steady himself. It was the same old pink page, with the same big cross made on it, and nothing else.

Shekhar realised that his shoulders were heaving, and his eyes wet. He was crying. He was back where he had started – clueless, helpless. The one clue he had, had turned out to be useless. A little fun had got him into this hell, and he had dragged Anubha and Gudiya into it. He was lucky to have Anubha – and how many times had he doubted her? And what a turn he had brought into Polomi's life. If only he could see her once, see how she was doing.

What could he do now that would set everything right?

He clenched his fist and fought back his sobs. This would not do. He would be careful. Wait, watch. Not trust anyone, be as alert as possible.

He got Sahdev to bring him a list of addresses of the whole office staff. The next day, he had visited each of their houses. By midday, he had tough-looking security guards stationed at home and at the office. By the evening, he had ordered a CCTV for the office. At dinner, he told Anubha about an imaginary business rival, and explained how she must make sure she made the best use of the security guard, for Gudiya's safety and her own.

All of this gave him a sense of being in charge. It was what he could do. But was it enough? As he lay reflecting, before drifting into sleep, he found himself sending a silent prayer: God, it's all in your hands. Help me now.

The next morning he was up early, as he had been these last few days. After breakfast, he headed straight for the Kali temple at Akashvani Chowk.

'Protector of the world, destroyer of evil, Mother', he mumbled in the sanctum, 'I trust in you, I ask you for shelter.' He found solace in the familiarity of it all: the redness of Kali's tongue, the din of the crowd, the haggard face of the priest, the overpowering scent of incense, milk and marigold. He thought about Polomi. 'Mother, take care of her.'

He felt lighter when he walked out. He even had a spring in his step.

A few days passed uneventfully. Life fell into its familiar rhythms. That evening, Anubha was in the mood.

'It's been ages since we went out, just the three of us', she pleaded. 'It's always with Sahdev, or the guard. Can't we be together by ourselves – us three? You drive, and we eat out?'

Shekhar was quick to agree. He was tired of the caged life. They were out in a few minutes, without telling anyone. It felt wonderful.

It was an evening to remember. Gudiya was chirpy, and Anubha radiated a happy glow. It had been a long time since he had heard her laugh loudly, shoulders convulsing and eyes crinkled. On the way back, Gudiya was fast asleep in the back seat. Anubha sat next to him, squeezing his shoulder once in a while, chatting away.

'Do you know, Triveni won't come tomorrow', she was saying. 'She will queue for her Aadhaar[1] I-card. It can even take two, maybe three, days. By the way, what about ours? I don't know when you'll get them. I've heard they won't give you gas cylinders without them.'

'Don't worry', Shekhar said, 'we'll get them all right. But yes, you'll have a hard time without Triveni. Do you want to get a temporary help for a few days?'

'Are you crazy?' This won't be the first time I haven't had help. I've managed before. But do get the bloody Aadhaar cards soon, no? Or are you planning to get them only after the folks at the Swaraj and Vasco da Gama Streets get theirs? Sometimes I think people like that are much more clued into the subject of officialdom than people like us.'

'What folks at Vasco Da Gama Street?' Shekhar almost shouted.

'What's wrong with you?' Anubha peered at him in the dark. She might have reacted more strongly if he hadn't got her used to his erratic ways by then. 'Don't you know?'

Shekhar mumbled a negative. 'Um-hm.'

'It's in Jagannath Para. The people there have just named all their streets. 1919 Street, Swaraj Street,

---

1. Identity card with a unique 12 digit number assigned to all the residents of India, and qualifying as a valid ID while availing various services like a cooking gas cylinder (Translator's note).

Vasco da Gama Street, and so on. They aren't official names, but that's the point. The *babus* weren't naming them, so they went right ahead themselves. It's a matter of pride for them. I heard about it from Triveni. And I like it. It's comforting, no, to see them aspire for more? And get it?'

'Aah, so that's where it is. I was just… I didn't know. It's a strange name to choose. So, do you tell Triveni about us? About where I'm going, and so on?'

'Do I know myself? And do I care?' Anubha said. She pulled his ear gently. 'I just have a faint idea. I know when you'll be back, of course… In any case, why would I tell her?' She was slightly louder now.

In that same instant, he felt as if he had got up from a long, restless sleep. He stretched his back, without changing speed.

'What's up?' Anubha asked.

'Does Sahdev live there as well?' Close to Vasco da Gama Street.'

'I guess so – he's the one who referred her to us, no?'

He had driven and trudged kilometres in this city, and the street he had been looking for was right next door. So, what if it was not on any map. And he did not need to be a genius to figure that the one who knew more about his trip than Anubha was Sahdev.

'I want to go to the Kali temple – is that okay?' Shekhar felt confident. 'I got some good news at work, but I couldn't go during the day.'

'At this time? The doors will be closed, no?'

'The gates will be closed. The doors are always open.' As he turned the car, he smiled at her with a confidence he had not felt for ages. He sensed that it made her happy.

It was a full moon night. The moon lit up the narrow street they were on. He could have made it without the headlights.

The Prison

Vivek Mishra

 FAINT LIGHT had diffused into edges of the inky dark outside. Maya got up from the bamboo chair and drew the curtain. She had spent all night in the hospital. Prashant was still knocked out from the intravenous sedative. His eyes were still shut tight after fourteen hours, but his eyelids seemed to quiver once in a while, as if his mind was at work.

Disease: unknown. Cause: unknown. Treatment: unknown. What next: unknown. All they told her was this: he thinks too much. He must stop. And what else could she say except that he couldn't stop? He had written all his life. About what was, what was not. He was an explorer of the jumbled jungles of thought. Prashant would steep himself so deeply in some subjects that when he came out of his exploration he brought back trophies of discovery – but left a part of himself behind. Now it was as if someone else had possessed his body. There was some turbulence below the still surface. His mind worked feverishly; the cross-questioning never ended.

The first signs began with his hair falling away with alarming rapidity. Then his nails turned green. When he woke up, his voice was gravelly. By the time he was in hospital, his hands had darkened. He hadn't slept for days on end, but his eyelids didn't droop as he read or scribbled. They tested all of his bodily fluids and tissue that could be tested. Nothing came of it. The doctors said it was an autoimmune disease. The body's defence system was responding to an unknown substance. What it was, they didn't have a clue. Whatever it was, it had unsettled his body, mind and soul. Maya felt helpless. There was nothing she could do except watch as Prashant's being fought the invasive substance as best it could.

At seven in the morning, the nurse told her that the doctor wanted to see her. Maya reflexively turned to the spotted mirror. It felt as if an invisible shadow had covered her face. Her dark circles had turned ugly. She angled back to look at Prashant from the door. He was still the same – unconscious, but not asleep.

It was true. A moving kaleidoscope of images was flitting past Prashant's eyes.

It was probably midnight. The emptied bottle of Indian-made 'Scotch' rolled back and forth in the gusts of wind that toyed with the doors. His body tingled and he gnashed his teeth as he eyed the bottle. He stared at the faint light outside the window. It had stopped raining from the sky, but once in a while the wind would shake the trees and release a minor shower from their leaves.

Prashant stood there, irritated at the thirst that had overpowered him so completely. There were three of them that night, Prashant, Tapan and Vikal. Vikal was six years younger than the other two. All three had their own cravings. Prashant wanted to know everything there was to know about the jail in South Africa that Tapan had gone off to explore, leaving behind anyone and anything that might have tied him down. Tapan's narrative had built up to a point where it was impossible to let him stop telling it. But Tapan would not talk any more without a cigarette.

'Well, if we're gonna get cigarettes', Vikal had said, 'we might as well get more whisky.' Prashant had tried to talk them out of it. The other two ignored him and Prashant watched on as they drove the battered Santro down the road from the guesthouse. He could discern the sheets of rain in the headlight beams.

He reflected on Tapan's stubbornness – the guy would go out at this time, in the rain, to get a cigarette. And he would buy a stick – and perhaps a spare – but never a whole pack. And one day, on a whim, he went off to South Africa, thousands of kilometres away, to an unknown island, to dig out stories that had been buried under the sands of time. He claimed he came back for Maya, but he did not even see her before he came to this guest-house on the hill with Prashant and Vikal.

What could Prashant tell Tapan about Maya and himself? Should he have said that he and Maya were living together as soon as Tapan, sucking on the Classic Regular – Milds was not for him – walked in through the door? That they were in love? Would Tapan continue his dark story in the same tone? Or would he step out for another cigarette and never come back?

Prashant had not told Maya about Tapan's trip to South America. Why hadn't Tapan been more eager to see Maya? What was he thinking? Prashant and Tapan had many things to talk about. They would not talk about them today either, perhaps. Prashant wanted to get the load off his chest, but that island, the jail – the stories of them came in the way. Were they for real? It all sounded fascinating, but Prashant could not tie it to his present. And what was the point of getting into something that happened in a South African jail during World War II? Was Tapan bent on reading from a page of history that history itself had wiped out? But then, the stories of the past that have been imprinted on our minds – especially when we were in our naive years – were written by the biased and the dishonest. Governments that were established by great leaders, with ringing slogans, flags and paeans to progress, stood by idly as the rights of the marginalised farmers, workers, artists and writers were trampled on, sacrificed to the so-called New World. And this new world, and its past and future…

A car horn blared. Tapan and Vikal were back. Vikal was like an excited kid when he slammed the door shut.

'Look what we got! Genuine hill country liquor! And the guy who sold it to us was even more interesting. He told us it used to be the first choice in these parts in the British Raj times. The white memsahibs, ladies, used to go for it over scotch', Vikal said. 'He started talking about his grandfather, who used to sing English songs to the tunes of local ones. It seems he had a thing going with a memsahib. We were in a hurry to get back, or he would have told us all about it. This granddad of his, he could read letters written in English in those days when people in these parts couldn't even speak proper Hindi. That guy had a lot of gossip, no, Tapan *Da*?'

Tapan was pulling fervently on his precious cigarette. He ignored Vikal's narrative. It was as if a dying patient was greedily gulping, Prashant thought. Tapan's face had relaxed, and his breath seemed less ragged. Vikal filled their glasses in no time. Prashant wanted to get on with the story, now that the other two had got their respective fixes.

'What I had discovered so far was heartbreaking', Tapan said. It was as if he had read Prashant's mind.

'The collective oppression that the world's artisans, artists, writers and poets faced, the dreaded diseases that spread from their exploitation, their struggles and deaths – these are not recorded in the histories of countries. These stories are buried with the inmates of that jail. Sometimes they flicker in the grey, fearful eyes of those who survived World War II when empires were collapsing from the impact of explosions on the skies and the earth. At that turn of history, in the smoke of confusion the forces of capital and markets had reared up. Some men and women of principle, who could think on their own and care for others, those who could create value, were wiped off the face of the earth. They lost not only the skills of their hands, and the scent of their lands, but the light of their eyes. Their own people gave up on them and marked them as dead. From far the corners of the earth, they were herded into that secret jail. They were told to record what they knew in their statements, and then forced to erase what they had written from their memories.'

'But they obviously spoke different languages', Prashant interrupted.

'Yes, so they first had to learn English. After that the process of squeezing out the knowledge in their minds would begin. Their minds would become feeble, until they were finally extinguished.'

Prashant felt sourness in his mouth, and a kind of thirst that could only be slaked by getting to the end of the story.

'What happened there was inhuman, of course', Prashant said. 'We can hardly imagine it. It seems it was a plan to suck out all original thought, to compile a thought bank for an unknown force. Once a statement had been extracted from the prisoner, an injection would turn him or her into a vegetable. If the statement wasn't forthcoming, or it wasn't valuable enough, the punishments were harsh and quick. Time became irrelevant for the victims. The process could last days, or months. The captors could force minds through cycles of extreme vitality and complete enervation. The captives wilted under this torture. The walls of their solitary confinement cells bore the scratches of their broken nails and snuffed out their screams with contemptuous ease. Some of them wrote out their anguish on the walls, but no one read those ramblings. Inexorably, their eyes turned to stone.

'For the guards, the prisoners were like fish in a pond owned by a sadist, who could snap a finger to electrocute his fish in an instant, and who kept them nourished just enough so that they would not die of starvation. The guards would make it a point to visit each cell, strip the prisoners completely naked and inspect them at leisure. They were probably estimating how many days the prisoner would last. They probably had bets going. After one such inspection the guards told their masters that some of the prisoners seemed to have a strange illness: their fingernails were turning green, and their voices had become gruff and machine-like.'

Vikal gulped his drink and put the glass down on the table. The sound rang in the room, and he posed with a finger pointing to the roof, as if to make an important point. Tapan looked at him, ignored him, and went on.

'No one seems to have figured who was really behind that jail, or what its final objective was. It might have been the global market of the future, or a different kind of empire.'

Prashant broke in.

'You know what', he said with a sigh, 'I've always had this feeling that what we think and understand is kind of guided by a script, a code laid down by the power behind a global market. It's as if our thoughts are second hand, they've already been read years ago. And we're living our lives out in robotic mode, under the illusion that we are intelligent.'

Tapan looked at Prashant with an intensity that was laced with more than liquor. His eyes hadn't lost their penetrating look. Prashant imagined him saying that there was much to talk about apart from the story of the jail. But when he talked, he picked up where he had left off. 'It's impossible to say what use was made of all the language, music, art and science that the controllers sucked away from the prisoners.'

Prashant said:

'Wait a minute. There's a lot of published research on the torture of POWs. How come this chapter never came out in the open?'

Tapan raised his eyes to the roof for a moment.

'Look, the average guy on the street sees what the select few with the remote control show him. And in 1939 to 1941, South Africa wasn't directly involved in World War II. Some South Africans were with the Brits heart and soul, but others saw the war as an opportunity to uproot the Empire from their soil. It was parts of Northern Africa, Ethiopia, Madagascar that were firmly in the war. That's one of the reasons for the location of the jail – this spot was far removed from all the big theatres of World War II.'

'But what about the locals?' Prashant asked.

Tapan flicked the ash from his cigarette.

'There's a ninety-year-old woman on Bird Island. She still works her farms eight hours a day. She maintains her father had discovered many natural remedies. He had also perfected a long-distance stringless bow. He would puff up his cheeks and use his palms to make the sound of a conga drum. Well, he was a bit of a whacky genius. He went out farming one day and never came back.'

'Hmm, like our booze shop friend's granddad.' Vikal butted in.

'It's possible', Tapan nodded. 'So the point is, many such people vanished at that time. Many of them were Indians.'

Tapan used the glowing end of his cigarette to light the second one he had bought.

'This old woman, she said that her father had impressed a German with his bow, and that he was taken captive by the Germans. Her younger sister doesn't agree, though. She says the Germans in South

Africa couldn't have had the resources to kidnap someone under British eyes.'

Tapan looked at Prashant as if he wanted to read his face.

'There's a lot more that I have to say about this. But there's also something else that I want you to know. Ant that has to do with you, and me. I have a question, and I hope you'll answer me honestly.'

Prashant's throat felt parched. He held Tapan's gaze as he took a big swig of his drink. Before he gulped it down, Tapan fired his question with a cloud of smoke.

'Do you love Maya?'

The liquor burned as it rushed in. Prashant's head swam. 'Yes', he said.

Tapan snuffed out the partially consumed cigarette on the floor.

⁕

Prashant was babbling inaudible words, trying to escape the clutched of the past, even as his body lay still.

Maya walked across to the doctor's room and stood in the doorway without a word. When the doctor spoke, it was as if he was talking from very far away.

'Look, we've talked to many specialists, but we haven't got anywhere yet. We will have to go ahead with what we've done so far – treat the symptoms.' He seemed to think for a while. 'In any case, your husband is too anxious. Once he has recovered, he will need a break. A trip will do him good. The way he is going, he will end up with a brain haemorrhage, if he doesn't slow down.'

Maya stifled the disappointment that welled up in her.

'Is he the first person in the world with these symptoms?'

The doctor sighed, and switched to a much softer tone.

'Well, I've never seen a case in which someone had these symptoms, with all – absolutely all – tests turning out negative. There's no kind of infection – viral, bacterial, fungal, nothing.'

Maya felt that she was sinking into a deep well and the doctor's words were bubbles at the top. She fought against the numbness that she felt herself slipping into.

'There must be someone, somewhere in this world who's had something like this?'

'There's no authentic report to go by', the doctor said. 'I've heard that in a secret jail in South Africa, some prisoners had these symptoms.' He spoke in a hushed tone, as if he was very unsure of himself.

'I knew it!' Maya screamed. 'I knew there was a connection to that bloody South African jail and to that cursed book.'

The doctor looked alarmed, and opened his mouth to speak. Before the words formed, a panicked nurse announced from behind Maya,

'The patient in room 3 is shouting in his sleep!'

Prashant was convulsing in his stupor, as if he was a prisoner banging his head against the walls that enclosed him, as if he had just lost himself in some ancient labyrinth. The doctor plunged an anaesthetic into him, and his jerky movements died out.

It was light outside. An intense rectangle of morning light had formed on the roof. The beam of light that led from the window to that rectangle lit up a thousand languid floating particles. Maya thought about Prashant's journey from his live wire days to this vegetable life.

Tapan had introduced Prashant to her. Prashant was full of stories. His anecdotes were endless, peripatetic. Tapan and Prashant had hit it off well. They seemed to have created a fantasy world for themselves, and Maya often found herself losing track of time as she listened to them. Tapan was obsessed with stories of suppression of rights, to the point of seeming to want to bring to light every such story that had transpired. Tapan the curious journalist and Prashant the thirsty writer – they were made for each other.

The moment Tapan learned about that jail was the turning point of his life. He became crazy about going there, even though he knew Maya wouldn't go. Maybe that was why he just slipped away without a fuss. Maya was used to his phases of obsession by then. She had thought he would get over with it and get on with his life. It turned out that she was wrong. He had always maintained that Maya could take care of herself. And then there was Prashant, of course. She sometimes thought that it was Tapan who had spun the thread that tied her to Prashant, only she did not know about it until Tapan had left. Maya never found out what transpired between the two of them after that.

For some time, she had this feeling that there was something enveloping her and Prashant. Like a thin, barely perceptible curtain. And then the curtain had shrouded her completely.

—◦෨෴෬◦—

Vikal came running up, rang the doorbell and barged in without waiting.

'Tapan Da's had an accident!'

'Where… when?' Prashant asked.

'Back in South Africa. He was on his way back to his room from a remote village.'

'But I just talked to him… day before yesterday.'

'So, you've been talking to him?' Maya felt rather ashamed that these were the first words that came out. 'And you didn't tell me', she continued anyway. She felt a nerve throbbing in her forehead.

'Yes, well, we used to talk. He was back in Delhi a few months ago. And he said he was about to send a very important parcel.' Prashant had talked in a toneless voice like he was completely in a fog.

While Maya was reimagining her past with Tapan, Prashant was already on to the future – he had a sense of foreboding. 'And how is he now?' he asked Vikal.

'How is he?' Vikal looked surprised. He looked away, slumped and said, 'He is dead.'

Each of them had much to say. Prashant and Maya looked at each other. Their words started to form, but didn't quite make it into the audible spectrum. Prashant walked into the bedroom in a semi-conscious state, and found himself seated on the floor.

The parcel arrived about two weeks later. It was a big cardboard box.

Prashant took the papers out one at a time, with the reverence that was due to Tapan's relics. A rich, layered narrative emerged as he delved deeper. There were handwritten anecdotes, statements from natives, copies of historical documents, sketches, photographs of drawings etched on plaster by the fingernails of prisoners… And most important of all, the diary of a mute native girl who was allowed into the jail.

Her name was Mattie, and she cooked for the death row inmates. These were the ones whose statements were complete. Mattie's speech impairment – and perhaps her ugliness – made her appear non-threatening to the jail officials. What they didn't know was that not only was she literate, she also kept a diary. Prashant never learned if she was alive, or how Tapan got her diary. But the diary had a note scribbled on the front inside cover, giving him permission to bring it into the light of the world. It was clear that Tapan had used the diary to plan his work.

Tapan had written, 'I can see the past, present and future. My landing up here in search of this strange case from the past may seem fairly unusual, but I am sure that what transpired here has shaped our fates.

'This evening, I went to the seashore Mattie has written about. Across the sea, on the island, I could see the black wall of the jail on top of a desolate hill. In the old days, the prisoners were taken to a field near that wall for a short while before being herded back into their dark cells. That was the only chance they got to see each other. They did not have permission to talk, or to shake hands. All forms of contact other than visual were forbidden. Some of them would stick their faces into the small square holes in the sea-facing wall. The guards thought they wanted to take in the sea breeze. Mattie knew that was the time when the local women would return from working the fields. The women would laugh at the prisoners ogling them; the prisoners would smile back since they could not make a sound. So it went on.

'There was an Afghan prisoner, a master cannon maker and a tambourine man. He would run to the fifth hole from the last one. One of the women, a tall beauty, always flashed a bright smile at him. One day, the Afghan had to fight another man for that hole. They broke the law of silence. When they stood there, panting, but smiling, the guards bayoneted him and left him standing there, hid head stuck in the hole, his smile frozen. He did not let the pain in his back mar his smile.

'When Mattie got home, her best friend told her the story of the woman sitting on the shore. She was in love with the fair man who looked out for her every day from the same hole. They would talk without speaking. It was better that way because they did not have a common language. They had decided to get married.

'Mattie frantically tried to explain to her that the Afghan was dead. Her friend did not get her. The women sang wedding songs and the one in love blushed and smiled. Her perfect teeth gleamed, her lips were full, her cheeks flushed. The full moon looked twice as big as it usually was. The clouds shimmered like a scarf that the waves had sent as a gift to the moon. The woman stayed there all night.

'Today I looked at that fifth hole for a long time. The sea breeze seemed to carry peals of laughter and sobs to me. I saw nothing, but I got a feeling that it was all happening right in front of me.'

Tapan's diary was full of stories of characters that had departed without sharing their deepest wounds, their suffocation. They oozed out of the diary and stood before him. They told him of their lives. At one point, Tapan wrote, 'Today I wandered all day and found nothing. I did get the feeling that someone was shadowing me. I was tired by the evening, and I parked myself on a small slab at the front of a giant rock. I noticed only after I sat down that I was surrounded by long-leaved bushes – the type that Mattie had mentioned in her account of the artisan from Dhaka who used to design carpets. He could see a carpet – any carpet in the world – and replicate it thread for thread without a second look. He made ineffectual attempts at designing carpets on the walls of his cell. He had used a blunt stone to etch out a map of the world in one corner. He had ticked all the countries in the world where his carpets had been sent. One day, he picked a piece of coal from the dark corridor that led to his cell. Mattie saw him do it. That day, when Mattie passed his cell, she saw him lying dead, flat on his face. She screamed a silent cry that no one heard. Mattie learned later that the guards who checked his cell in the late-night round had beaten him senseless because he had blacked England, America and Germany on his map. When the guards left, he blackened the whole map, and ate those long leaves. I felt a shiver as I sat there among the bushes.'

The sun had climbed to the window of the fourth-floor room. The small rectangle of light on the ceiling had expanded into a dazzling sheet of light. Maya was still lost in her thoughts. Someone knocked on the door. It was Vikal. Before he could come in and sit down, Maya said, 'I know those stories have done this to Prashant. They also killed Tapan. Trust me, before Prashant recovers, go burn those papers – the ones that Tapan sent, and Prashant's work. Throw the ashes into the gutter. Nothing good ever came out of those stories.'

Vikal looked at Prashant. He had got into the project half out of friendship, and half as a joke. By now, though, the stories had him in their grip. After what happened to his friends, he felt trapped like a character in them, like a character living out a script that was written in stone. There was so much he wanted to say to Maya, but she would flare up if he even got started. She didn't know that Tapan had returned from South Africa because he missed her. By that time, he had sensed that the powers he was working against had had enough of him, and could snuff him out any time. And then he got to know that Maya was happy with Prashant. He went off to the guesthouse on the hill without meeting her. Vikal remembered every detail of Tapan's story, and he felt that the pain of the prisoners had found its way into Prashant's delirium.

He had been collecting information about Prashant's condition, and had shared some of it with the doctor. He hadn't talked too much about it with Maya so far. Now he saw her looking all haggard and beaten, and couldn't stop himself from mentioning a newly released drug that a doctor cousin of his had told him about. It had just been commercially released. Maya looked at him with blank eyes. She had not really been listening to what he was saying until then. She brought herself to focus on his lips and the words he was mouthing started to make sense.

'I'm ready to do anything', she said. 'He must be freed.' Vikal saw that her eyes were moist. He averted his gaze. They both looked at Prashant.

Those sagas, their horrific endings and his strange illness had got Prashant in a vice-like grip, and his being had shrunken to a shadow of its past. He was discharged from the hospital two days later, and went to work with an impenetrable silence. Maya found the experience depressing. When she couldn't bear it any longer, she would pick up the phone and talk to Vikal, and ask him about the drug.

Vikal knew that it wouldn't be all that easy, and that Prashant himself would be the first obstacle. He had been told that the drug would release Prashant from his condition, but also erase all those thoughts that had stimulated it. He would lose the power to read and write and only have limited ability to think for himself. He would either lose the knowledge that he had acquired through literacy, or find strands of his knowledge congealed into a useless, entangled mass. He would live on, but be unaware of the past of his own body. He would never finish the story of the jail, and Vikal knew that was unacceptable to Prashant.

That evening he called Maya to tell her that the drug had been arranged. His friend had researched the topic for a long time. He was willing to try the drug on Prashant, but they would first have to get Prashant's consent.

What could Maya ask Prashant to do? Forget all he had known, learned, experienced, and live like a vegetable. It was a hard choice.

She sat alone in the drawing room, thinking of a way to engage Prashant in conversation. How had they ended up like this, casting shadows on each other? Prashant's smiling face and his eyes, dancing with life, had made her fall for him. She didn't even remember a particular instant when she left Tapan for Prashant, even while she lived with Tapan. She had found Tapan's quirky obsessions endearing enough for her to leave her hostel and move in with him. Once she met Prashant, Tapan's interests started to feel insipid. She often told Prashant that his stories didn't have the depth that Tapan's reports did, but it was Prashant's stories that played on in her mind long after she had read them. Now Tapan had departed, and his web of stories had enmeshed Prashant. True, Prashant's silence was a lot like Tapan's.

Maya made up her mind. She strode into Prashant's room and covered his eyes, which had been focused on a dirty map, with her fingers. The cool contact made Prashant close his tired eyes. She started talking about the drug. Before she could finish and ask Prashant to say yes or no, he gently pushed her hands away. She looked into his eyes. She knew that they were calm on the surface, but if she looked long enough, she would see them smoulder. His eyes were drowsy with the exhaustion of ages, but cursed to wakefulness by the fire inside them. Maya stroked his hair, and left the room, pulling the door behind her. She was exhausted and could not stand for too long. She collapsed on a stool in the corner. The silence in the room deepened. The needle of the old clock tried to break the silence, but it finally broke only at midnight with the voices coming from the bedroom.

It seemed as if Prashant was meeting the prisoners in person. He was talking to them. The prisoners' voices were hoarse. The babble of different languages echoed from the walls of the room, and the echoes combined to sound like a wail. The oppressive silence was shattered to pieces.

A quivering old voice said:

'Victory and defeat in the war, the millions of deaths – they were all set in motion by powerful forces. Capital doesn't only sponsor shows and competitions, it also sponsors war. It makes war hideous, and makes it last till its objectives are met.'

'And that's what happened then!' a thin voice shrieked, cutting in. 'The major powers played a dreadful game!'

'War was just a name for it', a calmer, gruff voice intoned. 'It was about owning land, and the natural riches of the land, it was about spilling blood to get absolute power. It was about sucking in all the wealth, thought and knowledge, and owning it.'

A trembling, but unexpectedly sweet voice said:

'When the colonies were crumbling, we thought we were getting freedom. But the powers had written a script to enslave the world. In this slave regime, minds and souls were bound by invisible shackles. You've read Mattie's diary, the incomplete diary. Mattie knew much more than she wrote. One night she saw Germans, British and some long-faced Caucasians – perhaps Americans – dancing together. That night, they didn't let her go after she had finished work. No one saw her again for a new decade.'

'Their clothes, their food, their technology is all ours. Stolen from us.' A controlled, gruff voice said.

Maya leant against the door frame. Something made her tremble with fear.

The voices joined in a chorus led by the gruff voice. 'Speak! You must speak, or everyone on earth will suffer the fate of those prisoners!' They were crying for justice, shouting cautions. It was as if they wanted to possess Prashant, and use his voice to spread their message to the world. They wanted his pen to become a weapon for their revenge. They wanted to be back on their own land again, to become part of its dust. To sprout again, to bloom, to wither. They wanted to be free in the earth of their roots.

Maya opened the door gently.

It seemed as if Prashant was clinging to the voices, tears streaming down his eyes, shaking with emotion, but also with conviction. For the first time, Maya felt that she was looking at a wounded soldier, and not at a tired, sick man. She went to him, took his hands in hers, and held him tight.

The rashes in Prashant's throat seemed to have eased. He looked up at the roof and said:

'The nailed soles of many boots have trampled me. My back is sore from countless lashes. My mind is the graveyard of the pains of thousands. But those people – they aren't dead! They are still banging their heads against the walls of pitch dark cells. I can't die, or live, until I liberate them.'

His head sank into the soft curve of her neck and shoulder. Prashant's head seemed to carry the weight of many heads. No one could have borne that weight alone. Maya realised how much Prashant needed her.

In the tumult of grieving voices, they held on to each other as they wept. Maya held Prashant's face in both hands and moistened his dry lips. His eyelids became drowsy. How many nights had passed without their feeling this relief, Maya wondered. She whispered into his eyes,

'Today the island of those stories is in us. Its walls are invisible, but they are everywhere. The jail has multiplied.

'Let's sleep for a while. Tomorrow, we'll work together.'

When Vikal came over the next day, there was a padlock on the front door. A chit peeped from it. Vikal unfolded it. It read, 'We're off. To free ourselves and all the others.'

The Case of the Bloody Future

Bhalchandra Joshi

HE WRITER DIGESTED HER STORY for a minute. He wore a dissatisfied frown. There's no detective in this story. No detection. Why insist on this title?'

She smiled her natural, sweet smile, with a mysterious twist this time.

'Hmm. There's mystery, there's suspense. Why don't you add the detection?'

'And you've told me what happened like it was a short story. Are you sure you haven't tampered with the plot a bit?' The lines on his forehead deepened.

'How would I tamper with it?' She was all innocence.

'You know how. You could have added or subtracted some of the details. How else?'

'Why would I do that? And Bhalchandra, weren't you in the story? You were an important part of it.' She had a way of modulating her tone so that she could tease you, lure you, without irritating you.

The writer felt beads of sweat form on his forehead. A trickle of sweat traced a path from above his ear to his right jaw. Her look told him that he might as well stop turning his spoon in his coffee cup – the sugar must have dissolved a while back.

'I want you to write the story your way', she said. 'If you feel like tampering with it, go ahead. It's all yours. But distance yourself from it. Write like an outsider.'

She sipped her coffee without making a sound. The writer felt embarrassed as he realised he had just slurped a bit. Her smile was mysterious, bewitching.

That is how she got this story written.

—◦⟨◦⟩◦—

'I don't believe stuff like that', she said.

He laughed out. There was no malice in his laugh, there was only clear laughter.

The winter evening was beating a retreat over the road, marshalling its troops into an orderly withdrawal. The forces of the night had not yet taken over completely, but a lull in the noise signalled that they were coming in. Through her shoes, she felt the road was already a little moist. Then she realised it was the air that was rather wet. It gave her a comfortable, tingling sensation.

They were returning from the jungle. He had told her that there was a ruined mansion in the jungle. A fakir lived in it, and he was famous for telling the future. A friend who worked in the theatre had told him about it. The fakir had the power to visit the future. He didn't use it for everyone. He was selective. If he felt like it, he could take a bystander with him, across the time barrier, into the future. The friend had told him the mansion was surrounded by many miles of forest. It was rumoured that the fakir kept changing his location.

'You mean like sometimes he's standing on a hill, and sometimes waiting by a river?' he had asked.

'No, he only gives audience in his mansion', his friend said.

'So?'

'So, he has this ritual of only giving audiences in the mansion… but the mansion shifts place within the jungle.'

He did not argue with the friend, but a bunch of arguments welled up and remained in his mind. When he took her there, he did not tell her the story at first. After they had trudged along for a long time, she finally snapped at him and asked him what he was looking for. When he told her, she recoiled and stood there ramrod straight, fists clenched on her hips.

'I don't believe stuff like that', she repeated.

He was all sweaty as well. He laughed, and meekly followed her as she beckoned him with an imperious movement of her index finger. They walked back.

When they reached the motorbike, he kicked-started it and sat astride it in a series of fluent moves. He moved his head to tell her to mount it. He drove fast. The signs of the city had not yet appeared when the jungle thinned out. The motorbike was rather strange. There was not much space on the cushion for the pillion rider. She wrapped her hands around his sides and chest. She knew that he would not say anything, but he was angry. She pressed her arms together tighter, as if to crush his displeasure with the pressure, to tell him that she wanted to fuse her body with his.

The wind that caressed the trees lining the road was energising, and the air was heavy with the dampness that would soon turn into dew. Her breasts warmed his back. The damp cold and her warmth created a chemistry that he couldn't figure. His unhappiness started to thaw.

He turned towards the coffee house at the edge of the city. Inside, they sat facing each other, still quiet. He broke the silence. 'It's nothing to do with believing or not. I wanted to meet the fakir and wanted to know what he sees in our future.'

'How does it help?' She asked, in a subdued kind of away. The vapour from the steaming hot filter coffee made her dark face gleam.

'Just curious.'

'Look, Angad', she said. She usually did not call him by name. 'Don't fool around with things that we don't know enough about after thousands of years of effort. First of all, we don't have a basis to trust them. And fingering the invisible lock that separates our world and the supernatural … it's just, I don't know – unnatural?' She frowned and looked into his eyes. He expected her to continue, but she did not.

He twirled the steel coffee cup, and said:

'With that thinking there wouldn't have been any progress in science. Mobile phones and video calls would still have been the substance of myth.'

'You're comparing science and superstition.' She leant forward. A wisp of steam still rose from her coffee. It disappeared into the tresses of her hair. 'If you did search for the future in a simulation model, I could buy your logic. But you're actually looking for it in the miraculous powers of god-men?'

'Nanda, this is typical Indian genius', he said. He did not usually say her name either. 'So, a scientist has to be a man, in a three-piece suit, in an AC lab? I don't know why we link science to a type of attire. If someone does research without wanting fame, cash, away from the establishment, can't it still be scientific?' He took off his thin-framed spectacles and put them aside, perhaps to show her the anger that still lurked in his eyes.

'Please! Don't link these fake god-men to science.' She spoke softly, but still conveyed her contempt. 'A true scientist will spend a lifetime on a single discovery or invention. These god-men – most of them just peddle sermons and amulets. They are frauds. Bandits. Society doesn't gain anything from them.' She stopped for a while. 'You know where their lust for power takes them? It makes rapists out of them.' She glared at him.

'You can't take one villain who's been in the news and paint all god-men in his light!' He was leaning forward, jabbing the air with his finger to make his point.

'No, ninety-nine per cent of them, okay? Ninety-nine. Ninety-nine point nine per cent of them are thieves, bandits, rapists. And finding the honest ones is as hard as visiting the future. And by the way, why are you all worked up about them? Look at you, brimming fire and all. You were never a religious nut.'

He slumped and looked away. He had this feeling that the argument had been steered so that he would end up looking like the obscurantist. In fact, he'd never been much into organised religion or its rituals. The desire to see the fakir had come out of nowhere – it could happen to anyone. True, he couldn't quite put a finger on what had possessed him to want to see the fakir so much.

He felt beads of sweat form on his forehead. A trickle of sweat traced a path from above his ear to his right jaw. Her look told him that he might as well stop turning his spoon in his coffee cup – the sugar must have dissolved a while back. He sipped the coffee and enjoyed its sweet, familiar, gentle burning.

They both liked the bitter sweetness of *kadak*, strong, coffee. This time when they left the coffee house, they carried its sweetness on their tongues, but their minds were burdened with the bitter aftertaste of their argument. Both of them felt lamely repentant. They knew that arguments like that one didn't lead anywhere, that such arguments were about taking a view and sticking to it. He dropped her off at home, and they parted with the agreement, sealed with half-hearted smiles, to meet at the theatre.

She couldn't sleep. Why did Angad want to know the future? Was it just curiosity? What if the picture was colourless, blurred … would they break up? It was a bit of a blow to think that a broken ruin in the jungle might hold the key to their relationship. And it wasn't comforting at all to think that the future was like a blueprint that existed somewhere – anywhere. Getting that blueprint would crush the pleasure of living in the present. It would reveal future sorrows and bring them into the present. So, the vision of the future that an unknown fakir showed in a crumbling ruin in the middle of dense jungle could be reliable enough to cast a pall of depression onto present. Did it make any kind of sense? Or was it a foolish way of paying to inflict pain on themselves?

When it all became too heavy for her, she jerked her head and pushed the thoughts aside. She resolved to get up then and study her lines for the next day's rehearsal, but she was too exhausted to move. She would wake up early and do them in the morning, she convinced herself.

He was not that troubled. He finished a basic dinner, and when he went into his bedroom he first went through his lines. As he lay in bed, he went over the day's events. She had really forced a useless argument. If she did not believe in that stuff, why be scared of it and why resist so much? She could have quietly seen whatever the fakir had to show, and then discarded it like a bad movie. But she did not. It was not her scientific temperament that had stopped her from going there. It was fear. What was she scared of?

There was something she was hiding that would come out into the open in that fakir's presence. Yes, that must be it. It was usually the girl who was more interested in the future, in the lines of fate. She was using her rationalism to cover her fear. He had a sinking feeling about it all. Before he could think any more, he sank into a deep sleep.

She woke up early, as she had planned, and practised her lines. When she came down, all ready to go, her mother had laid breakfast out for her. She devoured it, ignoring her mother's advice to chew slowly. She asked after her mother's arthritic pain and scolded her back for not taking her pills on schedule.

When she got to the theatre, she saw the rehearsal had already started. Angad came in just after her. After the first half, they opened their lunch boxes together. Her girlfriend Kanti joined them at their table.

Angad looked closely at Nanda, and was relieved to see that her expression didn't bear scratches from their fight yesterday. Her smiles were unadulterated.

She knew that he was scanning her for any signs of bruising. She felt a slight regret – his worry worried her. She kept mum. That's how it worked, she figured. If you wanted a preview of the future, you had to be prepared to sacrifice a little happiness in the present.

He tried to hide his unease. He made clumsy efforts to make it look like everything was all right. He insisted on bites of her lunch, without realising how unnatural it was to take her food. They always ate together, but they didn't share their meals. The whole group ate sitting together, in fact, but they respected the tradition of not pretending to be one happy family eating out of each others' lunch boxes. Space and time were shared, not food.

Her friend Kanti watched him without masking her surprise. Nanda and Kanti didn't have much to do after lunch. They sat back and chatted in the rear rows of the hall seats. Kanti poked her about Angad's foolish attempt to show everything was fine. Nanda told her what had happened in the last evening. Kanti turned sideways and looked at her with a tilted head and raised eyebrows.

Nanda shrugged. 'If you're with me', she said, 'I want to check that ruin out.'

'Yesterday you quarrelled about it – and today you actually want to go over?' Kanti said.

'Well, I slept on it. I wondered what Angad must have been thinking. And now I'm curious. I'm all fired up to go. If nothing else, at least we'll put this thing behind us. I can't let it drift, I can't stand by and watch him getting all flustered and acting strangely.' Her eyes narrowed and she pulled herself up to correct her slump. 'So? Yes or no?'

'He'll see us walking out, he'll ask us what we're up to. What will you say?'

'They'll be working till late today. Let's hang around for a while. We'll slip out towards the evening, and be back before the rehearsal is over.' She was decisive. She had already decided for Kanti.

Kanti had reluctance written all over her face as she nodded her assent. 'I'm just scared all this spy versus spy stuff will get us into trouble.'

Nanda held her gaze but didn't say a thing.

Kanti sighed and said:

'When?'

'We have the knife scene coming up, right? We'll finish that off, and then slip out. We won't go together.' She looked at the stage to watch the scene being played out. He was in it. He had stopped peering at them now. Now that they were all set to go, she felt relaxed and sleepy.

The afternoon sun had mellowed by the time they got out. By the time the scooter hit the mud road and settled into a different kind of drone, evening had started to creep up on them. They had to get off the scooter after a while. Its low wheels just couldn't take the ups and downs. And in any case, they had arrived at the exact point where Angad had parked the motorbike. They walked straight into the jungle, which was lit by a feeble but warm evening light. Even when it started to darken, it was very different from an urban darkness. There was the evening song of the cicadas with an overlay of birdsong, and the leaves and flowers still gave off signs of possessing colours that they could show off in bright light.

'*Yaar*, it's beautiful, this jungle', Kanti said.

'Yup. That's how they are', she said.

Her eyes were in the distance, seeking out signs that the contours of the jungle were familiar. She wasn't quite sure that they were retracing the path she had taken with him. Perhaps it was the raw beauty of the jungle that created an aura of a maze about it, and made it feel like a strange world each time you entered it. The trees were still, but the branches, leaves, and flowers rearranged themselves in infinite permutations.

She had lost track of distance. That did not help. She did not know how far they had to go. She did not say it, of course, but she had the feeling – more than once – that they had returned to a point they had passed earlier. The worn paths curved and banked so that she lost all sense of place. She wondered who had made them.

The sun had set, and the sky was covered by clouds. The clouds cast a shadow of deep black over the jungle. The darkness itself was soft and inviting, but it covered up small plants completely and it made the big trees appear hideous and menacing.

'I don't see a ruin. Actually, I see nothing.' Kanti seemed to be chiding her. 'Let's go back.'

Nanda stopped, and she sensed Kanti's relief. She hated to disappoint her but she had to. 'They say when you see nothing that's when you are very close to what you want to find', she said.

'Who says?' Kanti was anxious now. 'Where is it?' She grabbed Nanda's hand.

'Look, Kanti, this darkness is nothing. I've felt a weight on me since last night when I hesitated. I need to free myself of it. Come on, help me.'

She did have a sinking feeling that the trees were whispering to each other. The song of the insects had become background noise by now, but there were other sounds harmonising with it, and those sounds seemed to have meaning.

They walked on. It struck her that no one knew about their mission. Kanti's fear had somewhat infected her. She almost gave in – she would have told Kanti that they should turn back, the words were forming in her throat. Then she sensed a third presence on her right. She groped in the dark, but her hand didn't make contact with a body. It felt as if someone had dodged her fingers and was just there, just out of reach. She pulled Kanti to an abrupt halt. A deafening silence enveloped them. It felt as if someone had hit a switch to stop the sounds of the jungle from playing. Then the ground started throbbing, very softly at first. In a few seconds, it felt as if hundreds of animals were galloping past on both sides. It seemed like a stampede, and frantic rush that lives depended on. She stood there stunned.

'Did you hear that?' she asked Kanti. She realised her voice came out like a croak.

'Hear what? There's nothing to hear!' Kanti was still jittery.

Nanda kept quiet. The sounds of the thudding hoofs of the animals receded into the distance, and then were silenced completely. She had wanted to say they should go back, but her feet propelled her forward and Kanti walked with her, holding on lightly to her hand. She wanted to shout out, to say they should go back, but her tongue felt glued inside her mouth. She felt like screaming but her throat was numb. She was running now, and Kanti panted beside her, mouthing words that she couldn't decipher.

For a moment, just a moment, a bright light illuminated the jungle. Beyond a line of trees, she made out the outline of a mansion. Some of the edges had crumbled, but its white walls conveyed solidity, strength. So, this was it. A couple of seconds before, the mansion had been a dream. Now it was here, within reach. She ran, pulling Kanti with her. She ran sure-footed, as if she knew every inch of the path. It was less dark once they crossed the line of trees and the mansion loomed up ahead.

Its walls had cracks and gaping holes, but an impressive door with ornate carvings stood intact before them. A few of the windows and ventilators also survived. There were no trees within close range of the walls. She felt her feet dragging, and she had to think hard before she realised what was happening. They were walking on sand now. The sand was still warm, but she felt a chill as she looked around and saw rippled sand until the horizon on the far side of the mansion. She walked on into the mansion. Something made her lead Kanti through a hole in a wall, instead of using the door.

They were standing in a small room when she turned to Kanti, who was impassive beside her, probably too overwhelmed to react. She wanted to ask what Kanti thought about locating the fakir – should they shout?

He appeared out of nowhere.

He didn't look like a fakir. She had imagined him as a swarthy man with long muddy hair and an unkempt, knotty beard. A man dressed in tatters. Someone who looked like a fakir. He was tall, imposing, clean, bald-headed, and dressed in impeccable white clothes. He was smiling, but his eyes were cold.

'Don't look into my eyes', he said. 'Follow me, and don't look back.' He didn't wait for their reply. He turned back and walked away with measured, graceful strides. The girls followed him without demur.

'Don't you feel afraid here? All alone?' She asked him.

'Why would I be afraid, seeing I'm alone? In places that you inhabit, there's crime every day – loot, murder, rape. Don't you feel afraid there? Where is there more fear, there or here?'

She stopped herself from replying. She figured she shouldn't argue. She noticed that the mansion still had its aura of grandeur, although it had seen better times. Their path took them past an impressive staircase and a number of curving corridors. It began to feel like a labyrinth after a while. Again, she had lost all sense of place. Something seemed to be dragging her behind now, slowing her down, and the fakir seemed to be further away. She wasn't sure if the fakir had loosened his pull on her, but she pulled away from him and tried to turn back. She fell into a dark slushy space. It stank. It felt like she was in a big moat full of muck and water. She tried to steady herself and stand up, but it was slippery and she fell back again. She couldn't see what she was wading in, but it was smelly. It felt like a pool of blood and rotting flesh. She would have thrown up, but she had not eaten or drunk anything in a long time. She screamed. This time her throat was not numb, and the scream came out loud and clear.

A hand gripped her right hand firmly, and pulled her up. She was on a firm floor again. Her clothes were caked with slush.

'Was that ... was that blood?' She asked. Her throat was parched.

'I told you not to look back!' The fakir said. 'That was the edge of time. It has darkness and blood. That is how the past is.' His voice echoed in the corridor.

'Whose past? Mine? She asked.

'The past of our age.'

She didn't understand this at all. Why did she sense that he was smiling? She could only barely see his shape in the darkness.

'I'm bathed in blood! Is this blood?' she wailed.

He laughed, and this time the echoes seemed to come from many, many walls. 'Those who bathe in the blood of history have the guts to face the future', he said. He didn't stop laughing – he could laugh and talk at the same time. Something about his laughter told her he was sneering at her, and also warning her.

It turned darker. It took her a while to realise that it was because they were in a room with black walls. Where was Kanti? She felt her heart sink. She had completely forgotten about Kanti. Were the walls actually black, or was it just pitch-dark? She felt the whole room shudder. It was as if there were countless bats fluttering. She winced as she readied herself for a bat to fly into her at any moment. It didn't happen. And then, all of a sudden, there was a silence, as if all the bats had found their perches in the same instant. The quiet did not make her feel any calmer. She felt as if all the bats had their eyes trained on her. The deathly quiet was broken by a low noise.

It took a while for her to understand the noise. It was the commotion of war, of thousands savaging each other while with everything from swords to cannons. The war cries, the screams of anguish and pain, the calls to charge, the fluttering of flags… the horrendous soundtrack increased in volume until it deafened her. She could almost hear the thuds of falling limbs.

Nanda panted and wiped the sweat and tears from her face. She retched and almost collapsed. Again, a sudden quiet descended and stamped out the grating noises. It was a menacingly quiet. She could hear herself breathing now. Just when she thought she would control her breath, a plaintive chorus of weeping broke out.

Now it seemed as if thousands of men, women and children were crying. The sounds pierced her even more than the violent shouts that had been silenced a moment ago. Now the howling of wolves joined the weeping. The howls were punctuated by grating snarls. She imagined a thousand wolves in the mansion, looking up towards holes in the roof. Her eyes were itchy and rubbing made them worse. She felt drained. He ankles hurt like murder, and she could not stop the trembling of her hands even when she hugged her chest with them. She realised she had probably emptied her bladder – not that it made much of a difference. She could not cry, although a part of her wanted to. 'Was this death?', she thought. Would the wolves come and rip her apart? She could smell their stink now.

'I am dying', she said, in a tired, reedy voice.

'You are alive', the fakir pronounced calmly. 'This is yesterday.'

'But I wanted to see tomorrow.' Her mouth was dry.

'You have to look at the past to see the future. The more we forget history, the more blurred our vision of the future.'

She was about to collapse from exhaustion – or maybe die – when the fakir put his hand on her back. His voice became the only thing she could hear. It made her feel she was in a desolate place. She was still standing. It was quiet. She opened her eyes slowly. She saw that she was standing next to the fakir. He had a slick smile as he held a bundle of asters in his right hand. They had long stems. There is something wrong about them, she thought. This is not how asters are. But then it was pointless to think about what was and what wasn't.

The fakir gave the asters to her. It wasn't a gift-like gesture; it was more like he was handing her an heirloom. She didn't have anything to tie the asters. The fakir opened his closed hand with a flourish, to reveal a string of shells. He had read her mind. The shells weren't white – they were colourful. She tied the flowers with the string. She noticed the shells hadn't been painted. Their colours were natural. When she looked up again, what she saw made her want to scream. When she opened her mouth, only a strange wheezing sound escaped. Angad lay dead on the ground. His stomach had been cut open by a sword. His clothes were stained with dried dark blood. Someone she did not recognise came in and covered him to the neck with a white shroud. A stretcher lay ready next to him. Embers of coal emitted a wisp of smoke from inside a mud pot.

The scream materialised. Loud, heart-rending. The fakir held her hand in his. She used all the strength she could muster to wrench it away. His hand detached itself, but still clasped hers. She shuddered and used her other hand to free herself from the grip, and ran briskly. She did not think about the way out. She just ran without looking back. She got to the main door and fumbled with its rusty chain latch. She forgot that there were holes in the wall, and that she didn't need to worry about the latch. Then she remembered. She jumped through a gaping hole and landed on the front of her foot. The impact made her cry out. Kanti sat slumped on a crumbling platform.

'Where were you?' Kanti started. 'I...'

Nanda grabbed her hand. 'Run, get out!'

Kanti almost fell on her face. Her shoulder screamed with pain, but Nanda found the strength to keep Kanti on her feet stumbling along. She had lost her sense of direction, but she let her feet retrace their path back. The jungle path shone like a beacon in the black night. Soon, she was barefoot, not even aware when her shoes had been torn off. Out of the corner of her eye, she saw that Kanti had lost her shoes as well. The wild ground inflicted cuts and punches on her soles, but the pain seemed to stop there; her panic anaesthetised her. They weren't holding hands any more. They were running hard, and the harder they ran, the denser the jungle seemed to become around them. She heard Kanti's laboured breath and the thudding of the balls of her feet behind her. The headwind seemed to be like an invisible web that wanted to engulf them. She had lost all sense of smell.

When it seemed her lungs would burst, when her feet rebelled and the pain surged up through her knees, the jungle abated with a whimper. They were at the mud road. She knew enough to turn left on it. She recognised the familiar stretch where she had parked the scooter. It stood there, reassuring and beckoning. With trembling hands, she groped for the key in the right pocket of her jeans, which were still caked in slush. The key slid in, she turned the handle, and pressed the ignition. The purr of the engine made her cry. She pushed the scooter off its stand, mounted it, and only then turned back. Before she completed the turn of her head, she felt the motorbike tilt with a violent lurch, and Kanti's trembling hands grabbed her chest. Kanti's damp cheek was against her neck, and then she felt the wind in her hair and the scooter was navigating the contours of the mud road recklessly. They could have fallen. They could have died.

They reached the city, and then she drove slowly to the theatre. Or maybe it was time that had slowed down. They sat erect in the motorbike seat now. Kanti's hands were on the cushion. The building was dark, except for the usual faint lighting outside it.

There was a figure outside.

'Where were you both? And… what's happened to you?' It was the director, Chandraprakash.

'Where is Angad?' she asked.

'Umm…' his face fell. 'Leave the scooter here, and come with me.'

Her heart was thudding again. 'What is it? Tell me', she said as they walked towards his car.

Chandraprakash did not respond. He drove fast. Kanti held her hand and patted it. He led them straight towards the surgical wards. While they walked, Chandraprakash said a few words that Nanda could not understand. He led them to a ward with a big crowd waiting outside. All of Angad's family were there, and the whole theatre group. She ran into the ward. She only distinguished one of the patients. He was covered with a white shroud. It had to be Angad.

She saw the glass beading on the floor and felt a jarring pain in her elbow.

⸺◦⟨⟩◦⸺

When she opened her eyes, she was in an unfamiliar bed and the roof looked very distant and dirty. It took some time – she had no clue how much – to recall everything that had happened on her journey to this hospital bed. She sat up in a panic.

'Hey, relax. Get back to the horizontal mode', someone said, and she loved the sound. She saw it was Angad.

Her eyes were moist. He wiped them with his finger.

'So? How do you feel?' he asked.

'Me? What happened to me? You say! That wound in your stomach…'

Angad patted her shoulder. 'Just be quiet. You need to rest.'

'But I'm okay. I saw your… I fainted.' She looked around. 'Did I fall too hard when I saw you in the hospital?'

'Me? At the hospital? No, something went wrong when we were rehearsing the knife scene. We're not sure what happened, but the prop didn't work, and the knife went into Kanti's stomach. She's still unconscious. You both were sitting too close to the edge of the stage. You fell off, and got a knock on your head. Luckily you broke the fall with your other parts, or… Anyway, you both have been here since yesterday afternoon.' He got up from her bed and walked to the chair beside it. 'Kanti… she's still not conscious, but it seems she will be okay.'

She must have looked disbelieving.

'What? You don't believe me?'

She reached out for his hands, and he put his hands in hers. She wanted to hold them tight, but she was too weak. He pressed her hands gently, and caressed them until they stopped trembling.

She let it all out. She babbled out her incoherent, fantastic story of the events that led to her fall. He listened attentively, keeping an expressionless face. His eyes wanted to widen, to express disbelief, but he controlled them. Only at the end, he threw his head back, and laughed a soft, polite, long laugh. He caressed her forehead.

'You've hurt your head worse than the doctor thinks. You need to sleep again. Like I said, yesterday afternoon is when you landed up here. I called your parents. They've just stepped outside for lunch.' He had his fondest, most refreshing, most reassuring look. He couldn't be wrong, she thought.

Her parents visited her, and later a throng of friends from the theatre group. They looked happy to see her talking normally. When she was left alone with him and her parents for some time, and they were quiet, she tried to piece it all together. Yes, it must have happened the way he said it. This could not be another dream. The one with the fakir must have been the effect of the sedatives. She wished she had not told him that adventure story. She asked for water. She could not get up on her own, although she tried to. He cranked up the upper half of her bed, and turned to pour water out of a thermos.

From her new viewpoint, she saw the flower vase on a table in the corner. It had asters in it. Their thin stems were tied by a string of shells. The shells weren't white – they were colourful. Their colours looked natural.

She felt a gust of air. She must have screamed, although she did not know it. She fell back on to the bed from her slightly raised position. He ran to her. The nurse was there almost immediately, and the doctor came in very soon after.

She was unconscious again. The doctor gave her an injection himself. She was deep in a peaceful sleep very soon. The nurse scribbled something on the chart that was clipped to the backrest.

As he turned to leave, the doctor patted Angad's shoulder. 'She'll be all right soon. Don't worry.' Angad nodded and smiled.

He sat down on the chair in the corner. After a long time, the lines of worry on his forehead melted away. He looked at her with a gentle smile that lit up his face. He was smiling, but his eyes were cold.

Chess Pieces

Nivedita Jena

T DID NOT LOOK GOOD. Nita had to get to Rourkela soon. Her son Ujjwal was not well. She had not seen him for two weeks. She had been busy with the film shoot for ten days, and for five weeks, she had drowned her sorrow at being chucked out of the film. She was proud of being a great actor. That was how she was known in the world of theatre. When she got a chance to act in a film, she leapt at it. She left her four-year-old boy with her sister and marched off to the shoot. But it did not work out. Such was life. Just when you thought life was giving you a good deal, it handed you a rotten tomato.

Her passenger train was stuck at Jharsuguda station, platform number 2. It had been two hours already. A 'superfast' express, that would do

80 kilometres an hour, thundered onto platform number 3. Nita's fellow passengers eyed it through the grimy glass panes. Nita smirked to herself as she thought they looked like beggars looking at a posh socialite.

'That Rourkela Express will take them there in two hours. We won't get there before nine at night', a thin, gloomy man said. No, she could not rot here. She had to move, fast. She pulled out her suitcase from below a smoking man's seat. He moved away politely but did not offer to help. She realised how weak she had become after fifteen days of erratic rest and cheap food. The coolie had taken the suitcase up from the boot of the taxi all the way to the slot under the seat. Now it hurt her shoulders back to drag it off the high steps of the passenger train, on to the platform and across towards the express.

That was when the steel wheels of the express train started to squeal. Her knees and shoulder screamed in protest, but she managed to lug the heavy suitcase and herself up the ladder and into a coach of the super-fast express.

In the dim light, she made out the caretaker sitting cross legged in his seat, dressed in the standard shabby grey uniform. Before she boarded the train, she had noticed in the writing on the glass windows that it was an AC coach.

'Madam, where are you going?'

'*Ji*... Rourkela', she said, prefixing the honorific by reflex. She was still panting and she knew she shouldn't have walked in without a ticket.

'But this goes to Bilaspur, not Rourkela.'

'What?' She could have banged her head against the plasticky wall. The train had picked up speed by now, and the sloping edge of the platform disappeared as she looked back. She stopped herself from bursting into tears, and asked, 'Which is the next stop?'

'Bajrajnagar', he said.

So, she would have to come back to Jharsuguda and then start from scratch for Rourkela. She had two more connections to worry about. Nita felt like jumping off the train. She imagined the rush of air and the plunging feeling in her heart.

'I suggest you go to a sleeper coach, madam. The conductor is very greedy. He'll want to be greased, or slap a big fine if he finds you here. He will go to check in the sleepers after Bhubaneshwar, and by then, you will have left.'

'Which way are the sleepers?'

'Both ways, at the ends. You can go either way.'

Nita had not expected this reply. All the attendant had to do was point a finger left or right, and she would have followed the direction. His reply pushed the burden of choice on her. All she had been doing for the last few weeks was asking people questions, and letting their answers decide things for her, without thinking too much about how true they were or what lay behind the answers. That was how she had achieved the distinction of becoming a film actress – she had more or less stumbled into it. And then, the humiliation of being sacked even as her histrionic skills were praised, the shock of being left behind when the crew went for a shoot, the numbing discovery that someone had taken her place… What was it that she had not done right?

'Sir, I've been here twelve days', she had grovelled as she spoke to the director, Arjun Mahapatra. 'My son isn't well. I'm going through a rough patch. And you choose this moment to chuck me out? This isn't right.'

Arjun Mahapatra gave her a stony look, as if he did not want to expend any emotion. He did not say a word, but it was clear the look meant he did not care. There was nothing she could do about it – and they both knew that. He was a big name, and they had not bothered with the formality of a contract. He did not look troubled by what he had done. Nita was out of the scene as if she had never been there. She was too stunned to kick up a storm. She had paid the price for trusting the informal work arrangement, for assuming she would get humane treatment. Now the trust was shattered, and her confidence in her acting ability had waned. It reminded her of her teenage years, when in bad times she would ask if there was a god, and what he gained by putting her through ordeals.

Nita thanked the attendant and walked left. As she opened the thick door that separated the air-conditioned part of the coach, her mind had already half-formed the image that would present itself. There would be a long corridor, crossed by aisles and partitions. It baulked at what she saw. There was just one big coupe in the whole coach. A dim blue light came from the coupe door, which was ajar. Nita walked past it towards the other end. Before she crossed the threshold, a tall, well-built, completely bald man opened it and stepped out. In that dim blue light, she could just about notice that he was very pale-faced. She reached up to his chest. His eyes were a dark colour, and so was his coat. She could not make out in that filtered light what colour it was.

She controlled her breath. It was the key to fighting fear.

'Excuse me', she said in English in what she hoped was a matter-of-fact tone. The man looked like a foreigner, a Caucasian.

'*Andar aa jao*, come in', he replied in Hindi.

'I need to go', she said.

'Where?'

'Rourkela. No, I mean to the next stop. There I...'

'What? Do you want to go to Rourkela or not?'

'I do, like I said. But I got into the wrong train.'

'Who says?'

'What do you mean? Isn't this train going to... the other direction?'

He took her suitcase and pulled it in. She followed him without a word, as if she did not have a choice.

'Sir, will this train go to Rourkela?'

He slid the steel bolt of the door shut.

Her heart was fluttering. What a fool she was. Why had she followed him in?

He held gripped her shoulder – in an asexual way – and forced her down onto a seat. It took her a while to figure what was strange about his touch. It was ice cold. As she sat there, she realised she had goosebumps. It was way too cold. She pulled the curtain aside, but before she could take in the view, the light-skinned man shouted,

'Pull that back!'

She obeyed him like an automaton. How had she landed into this? How could she get out? She calculated how much time it would take to jump up, pull the suitcase out from the upper berth where the man had tossed it, run for the door, open the bolt, and…

'I won't do anything to you. Sit back, relax', he said. He picked up a drink from a tray next to him, shook it and took a swig. 'So, you're Nita. I am Satan', he said.

Nita did not know what to say.

He smiled.

'Your name's on the suitcase. Common sense.'

Why the hell had she followed him here? How would she ever get out?

'What's surprising about it? Don't you always let others decide things for you?'

She gulped. Was it her mind he was reading? Or was that a comment on women in general?

'What is it with you girls?' the man called Satan said. 'Why don't you exercise your minds? Your father decides what you'll study, your brother decides what job you'll do. Or maybe the in-laws, later. Your husband lays down the dress code. How many kids? The government will tell you – or the consumer price index. Whom will you marry? You can't cross the religion fault line. Oh, and who will you love? The biggest master of all, society, has to stamp its approval. So, what are you? Aren't you all puppets?'

'Not me!' She said firmly.

Then she realised it was just a thought – she thought she had said it. She knew he had fingered a sore spot. She had been brooding for days on end about how the decisions she saw as her own – while making them – were made for her by others.

Satan's shoulders and head were jerking in slow motion. It took her some time to realise that he was laughing. He convulsed silently for a while before he let out the guffaws. She almost collapsed when she saw his teeth. They were big, really big, and sharp. His incisors were fearsome, like an animal's. She looked at his drink. It was dark, like the blood she had seen in pouches in hospitals.

She was on her feet.

'God, where have I landed up?' She said. She looked into his eyes and held his gaze although her hands were trembling. 'I have to go!'

He stood up and drew himself up to his full height. He came closer and stood touching her.

His smile was pleasant, and his teeth were hidden again.

'You'll go, later. We're not done yet.'

'No, I'm going!' She moved back. She would leave the suitcase there. She figured she had her money and her mobile in the black vanity bag on her shoulder. She felt weak, helpless, drained. But she was also trembling with rage. She closed her eyes, focused her fury, and pushed the man.

He was surprised enough that she could turn around and step towards the door. But he grabbed her from behind in a second. His grip was like a vice. Her arms hurt, and her eyes watered with the humiliation. Would he rape and murder her? She would never see Ujjwal again. God, save me this once, she prayed. You've played with my life until now – this time, save me for my son's sake. She screamed in protest.

The man did not relax his grip. He purred into her ear:

'I'll let you go. But why don't you meet the one you've been thinking of, before you go?'

So, he had a game plan. He must have kidnapped Ujjwal.

He let go of her. She turned around to face the towering man.

'Where is my son?' she asked.

He pointed a finger to the berth where he had also put the suitcase.

She climbed on to the lower berth, and steadied herself with the steel belt that supported the upper berth, to get a look. A small boy of four lay there. He was about Ujjwal's age. He was dark, and he lay with his face turned away. He wore a cream shirt and matching dark-brown shorts. He had used his bent, thin left arm as a cushion. He turned towards her in his sleep, and opened his eyes. He gave Nita a dreamy smile. She got down quickly.

'That is not my Ujjwal', she said.

'Ah, is that so? Then I shouldn't have detained you', he said. 'You can go.' He strode to the door and opened it. Nita hadn't expected freedom to come so easy. It was such a relief that the man hadn't kidnapped Ujjwal. She climbed on the berth again, and took her suitcase, struggling under its weight. Out of the corner of her eyes, she saw tears in the boy's eyes. She felt a choking sensation. What were his parents going through? She pushed the suitcase back, and reached out for the boy's hand. He smiled through his tears and extended his small hand towards her. The man who called himself Satan moved lightning fast. He gripped her arm and pulled her down. She collapsed on the floor, and she felt a shooting pain in her left ankle. She hobbled up.

'The boy isn't yours. Go!' He said.

'Whose boy is he?'

'Go.' The man's eyes were red. His voice was soft.

'Whose boy is he?'

'It's your life!' He exploded, and she felt like crying.

He reached behind his back and when his hand came back into view it held a silver pistol. She had to clench her muscles to stop herself from wetting her clothes. She thought of Ujjwal. She must go. If she lived, she could report the case to the police. She climbed up again, getting her right foot to take her weight, and reached for the suitcase.

'Don't leave me', the boy whimpered.

She should not have looked into his eyes. She lowered herself again, and sat down on the berth where she had sat before.

'Whose boy is he?' She asked. Her voice didn't tremble this time. She felt cold and tired, but she had lost her fear.

His face twitched. He sneered and his eyes pointed to the pistol. It made no difference to her this time.

The sudden urge to pee had receded. She did not know what to do, how to get out of there with the boy. She needed to buy some time.

'Whose boy is he?' She asked again.

'You're crazy! Stupid woman, Ujjwal is sick. He's waiting for you. What kind of mother are you? Cruel and insane. You're leaving your son in the lurch for that boy there, whom you don't know? What will you get out of it? You're the kind of woman who would do anything for money and fame. But this – this is stupid.'

She hated it when her eyes became wet at times like this, without warning. Was he right? She felt hopeless again. But then her anger took over. She figured that even if it was not Satan in front of her, it was an evil man who had taken the trouble of finding out everything about her. That was all there was to it. She should not fall into despondence so easily. No, she would not leave that boy to a horrible fate.

'Whose boy is it, damn it?' she said. This time, she resisted the urge to shout. She spoke softly, looked up at him, and drew out her words.

He did not flinch, but he showed that he knew something had changed in the nature of their interaction.

'Mine. He's my brother', he said.

'What? Have you kidnapped… How can he be? He's so much younger!'

'No, he isn't. He waxes and wanes like the moon.' He snapped a finger, and the boy quietly climbed down.

Nita could not believe it. He had lost his childlike sweetness. He was almost as tall as her now. He came up to her forehead. His face had thinned out, and his lips had changed their shape. His eyes had sullenness about them. She felt as if the rhythmic throbbing of the train had stopped for a second.

'Oh God!' She blurted out.

'That's him', the man said with a smug look.

She did not know what to say. It seemed as if there was a small part of the planet in which the laws of the world did not apply, and she was in that part of the planet here in this coach. God, oh God.

The boy was sitting up now, looking at her. 'I am he', he said. His voice was soft. She was scared of him now, this cherubic boy for whom she had stayed back and risked her life. She realised she had not even taken a good look at him.

'Who – how old are you, son?' She asked him. It had been a long time since she had really questioned someone, and now it would seem she had questioned both Satan and God.

'I don't know. Some millions of years, I would guess', the boy said.

'What?'

'Yes. In the beginning, before the earth, there was no life. There were no humans, of course, there was no vegetation. When I awakened my powers, the universe resounded with the holy chord, Om. From algae to *peepal* tree, from moth to man, I created infinite nature. There was light and happiness everywhere...' The child god had become more imposing and confident. But then he stopped for a moment, as if he was readying himself. 'Then I noticed that one corner of the creation was still dark. I had to erase that darkness, to complete it. But I couldn't–'

'Complete it?' Satan interrupted. 'How can you end something that never began? Fool! There was darkness before there was anything. You just said it. And I exist with it.' He drew himself up to his full height, and folded his hands. From the innards of her twisted memories, words came floating into Nita's mind: 'Before light there was darkness, before virtue sin, before life death...'

'Yes. That's exactly it', Satan said. 'That's exactly how I am older than this god of yours, greater than him.'

'You are older, but not greater.' The child god was loud and bold now.

'It doesn't matter what you think. It's what people think that counts. They know by now that it's foolish to be honest, simple, true. That's the thing. You've completely lost the battle. You say: "Do your duty without the desire of reward. Stay on the true path even in the face of hardship". And what do people say to that? Bollocks. They switch allegiance to me.' His speech was measured, silky, confident. It seemed to Nita as if God knew that he could not sentence Satan's followers to punishment in hell. He was constrained by being kind and merciful. He was known to be forgiving. He would wait until the final hour for those who had strayed to return to his fold. Satan stood there mocking him, as lines of worry formed on the child-God's forehead. It looked like he was aware of the mass desertion of humankind, and it had broken his heart.

Nita ignored all this. She addressed the child. 'God, why do you appear so small. Is this man true? Does your age wax and wane?' She noticed how handsome he was. He was dark, and his face seemed chiselled and exuded innocence. He looked like a supremely talented *Gottipua*[2] dancer, a being that

2 . *Gottipua* is an ancient dance form of Orissa (a state in Eastern India). Young boys dress as girls and perform for the Lord Jagannath. It is said that they take the feminine form because only in that form is there complete submission to the Lord.

exhibited the feminine traits of love, tolerance and flexibility while residing in a man's body.

'Yes, it does', he said. 'My emotional state is a function of the state of my creation, and that reflects in my strength and apparent age. When creation suffers cruel attacks, my strength starts to recede. It's worse when my most accomplished creation, humans, harm their own environment…' He looked pensive as he stopped for a moment. 'But thank you', he continued. 'If you hadn't stood by me when you did, if you hadn't put yourself in trouble for an unknown child… I wouldn't have been stronger and older, as I am now.'

Nita felt a lightness she had never experienced in all her life. She had chosen, chosen right, and her choice made a difference to God.

'I'm getting bored', Satan said. 'Let's start a new game.' He sounded impatient.

The child-God looked troubled.

'Let's try a fight', he said and his face broke into a sneer. His teeth showed, and Nita shuddered. He locked his fingers behind his head, cracked his knuckles and flexed his muscles.

The boy lowered his gaze.

'What? You can't do it? You surrender? So, you do admit I am greater?'

'No!'

Nita was breathing hard.

'God, get down, stand up to him! Defeat him and banish him from the human world, just as you did from heaven!'

'I will fight him only on equal terms. Right now, I am fifteen and he is… you can see. Someone, somewhere, must do something that makes me stronger and older… then I can fight.'

'What can I do?' Nita asked.

'You are a woman. Imagine you have all the power of a woman in you. The infinite power of mother, wife, lover, sister, daughter. Decide what form of warrior you want to see me as, and give me the power to take on that form.'

Nita walked over to him, and he climbed down from the berth. They ignored Satan. She hugged him and kissed his dry lips.

'I gave you all my love. I want to see you battle him. I will be with you even if you lose.'

She felt herself crushed in an iron grip. Yes, it was him! He had morphed into a strong, radiant man, much taller now.

'I am proud of you, of my creation', he whispered and kissed her forehead.

'Hmm', Satan sneered. 'So, there's a lot of tender love between you both. Okay, I've chosen my weapon. This woman will be our test of skill. Let's see if your godly love can beat my satanic moves.'

'I'm not a pawn for you to do as you like with me… A human life is not a die', said Nita. A vein was throbbing in her neck.

'Oh a human life is the best die, I assure you – and a woman like you is best suited to be a pawn. You'll see, we will play the game, God and

I. How about it, God?' Satan said. He was loving this.

God nodded his assent. He said he would play first. Satan shrugged and wandered to the window in the corner.

'God, why me, all over again? You've just had me sacked by that bloody Arjun Mahapatra. Now this… Let me get home! I'll – I'll support you from the outside, of course.'

'Don't be like a politician', God said. 'First of all, I'm not the one who chose you. Second, there's no one else here whom I can trust. At least for now.'

God needed her. That sounded good to Nita.

'You're bound by your rules, but does Satan have any that he plays by?'

'Satan's primary rule is that all rules are meant to be broken.'

She looked around and saw that Satan had slipped out of the coupe. Then she saw God was looking at her. He leant in and kissed her lips in a chaste way. He looked serious.

⁂

Nita felt tired and sleepy. She jerked her head and forced herself awake. There was something strange about the way the floor was moving. Actually, it was not. She was on grassy ground. She was in the middle of a jungle. What was all this about? Was this god's move? A soft evening light filtered through the dense foliage. She felt dizzy as she took all this in. It looked like the sun was satisfied with a job well done, and thought it was time to laze a little.

Nita was a town girl. When she was small, her parents would take her every summer to their village during the Raj festival, the festival of swings. As for jungle – there was not much of it in her life, except for what she saw on National Geographic channel. From school, they used to have outings that the school would bill as 'forest picnics', but they entailed finding a convenient spot to eat in the nearest grove of about a dozen-odd trees.

Now here she was, in the jungle – for real. She looked around and saw a small hill not too far away. She figured she would get a good view from there, and perhaps spot a way out, or a sign of habitation. The bare, red hill rose more than a hundred feet above the trees. She panted as she walked up its slope, and a few times, she stopped to catch her breath.

When she finally got to the top, the view helped her forget her pain and enervation. A green carpet of trees surrounded the hill. After she looked for some time, the green decomposed into an impressionist pastiche of many hues. The canvas of darkest green was sprinkled with smears of a golden-hued lighter green, bursts of yellow from golden shower trees and brilliant red from royal poinciana. Above the horizon, a few golden white wisps of clouds decorated a clear blue sky. The changing shades of the clouds reminded Nita that the edge of darkness would soon race over the horizon.

A roar brought her back to firm ground. It was a tiger or a lion – no, wait… there were no lions in these parts. Whatever it was, it might have let out the roar as it pounced on its prey. From a gap in the canopy of trees, a flock of birds fluttered up noisily. Nita realised that the beauty of a landscape that could have been featured on Nat Geo was all very well, but she needed to figure out a survival plan for the night. It struck her that the hill was fairly strange. It stood there completely bald, right in the middle of dense forest. It was as if someone had shaved off all the vegetation from there. She walked around the hill, and came to a rough mud platform with a small hole in it. She could get into the hole, and only her head would project out of it. She only had to duck a bit, and she would be hidden. What was this platform for? Could it be a religious altar – and the hole a place for sacrifices? A shiver ran through her, and she cursed her imagination.

From a distance recess of her memory, she recalled a TV story about someone who had climbed up a tree to survive the night in a jungle. That was what she must do, she figured, but here was a minor problem – she had never climbed a tree. Well, it was never too late to learn. She must find a tree with enough branches to climb on. Her calves hurt as she walked down the hill. She wandered for a long time.

'God, couldn't you have put in a climbable tree or two?' She shouted out aloud.

She felt guilty at disturbing the peace. Then an elephant's trumpet made the ground and the air vibrated. Now she was really furious at God. What kind of game was this that he had got her into? Why did she have to be in this jungle full of lions and elephants? She, whose closest contact with wildlife, until now, had been buying 'Save the Tiger' stickers from schoolchildren?

Couldn't God have dispatched her to a jungle without deadly predators? She would have been okay with deer and rabbits.

The sun was speeding towards the skyline now. The shadows of the trees were lengthening and merging. She looked back towards the hill. When it became dark, she would be able to see fires lit by people close by – if there were any people close by. Still, it was worth a try. She trudged back up the hill. Her throat was completely parched now. It hurt when she gulped, and a masochistic instinct made her want to gulp again and again. She walked around the top of the hill, panting, looking for signs of smoke or fire. There was nothing. She wanted to call out to God, to ask for water, food, shelter. But what was the point?

She was hungrier now than she was thirsty. And the air had turned cold. It wasn't biting cold yet, but it was bad enough. She realised what she needed most of all was fire to warm and protect her. She walked around and picked up dry sticks. Pretty soon, she had assembled a rather big bundle. What could she light them with? She didn't have a lighter or a matchbox. She made a mental inventory of her vanity bag. A small mirror, lipstick, articles for make-up, cash, debit card, visiting card, credit card, mobile – all of those things which she would never leave home without. None of them were of any use now. Her hand wandered to her bag, rummaged inside and came out with the mobile. No coverage, as she had expected. It was just a piece of plastic. Then she noticed a message in her inbox. She opened it.

'Join me', the message said. 'You'll get food, water, a warm room. And more – you'll have a good time in a silvery, romantic night. You know who I am.'

God had shunted her off to this godforsaken place. Why should she care for him? Why not join Satan? She imagined herself in a warm room with a fireplace, enjoying the view of the silvery night outside. Then she thought of the feeble god she had seen first, the one who had pleaded, 'Don't leave me.' No, she couldn't switch sides.

She looked around. The ground was strewn with brown and black stones. Was one of them the type of stone, which, according to Nat Geo, would produce sparks of fire? She picked up a pile of different types of stones, and got to work with them. Pretty soon, her fingers were mauled and her hands were aching. There was no trace of fire. Finally, she was overcome with grief, and she burst into tears. The path of good certainly was not the easy one.

The steady din of insects was punctuated by the periodic cries of animals. It would be pitch-dark very soon. She must have fire! She cursed her weakness, wiped off her tears and got back to work on the stones. She picked up a few leaves and tried different combinations of stone. She almost could not believe it when the first spark came out. She almost cried with relief. Soon she had to rush around to collect enough dry leaves to keep the fire going. A couple of sticks caught fire, and she sat there basking in the glow, feeling drained and proud.

She got up to scour even firewood to last through the night. She walked towards a part of the forest she had not been to earlier. This time, just a few feet into the forest, she found a bundle of wood tied together neatly with the stem of a plant. It looked like someone had collected wood, but had left it there in a hurry. She thanked God. It was heavy, but she managed to drag it to the hilltop.

Soon, she had relieved herself in a corner, and arranged a ring of fire around the hole in the ground. She was still thirsty and hungry, but she was full of optimism now. She sank into the hole and leant back. It was not plush, but it was comfortable. It was nice to feel that she would live to see tomorrow. And it was God who had seen her through the hardest part of her ordeal.

On the other hand, now that basic survival was taken care of, her mind wandered with increasing intensity to thoughts of water and food. What could she do about them? Going into the jungle and foraging for them were beyond her, much like scaling Mount Everest. Or maybe not. She levered herself out of the hole, hopped across the ring of fire, and walked into the forest. Ah, if only she could find a fruit tree in the little light that remained…

She walked on for some time, using one bright star and the moon as navigation aids. She had no luck with the fruits. She was about to give up and turn back, when a shrub rustled and a beautiful cat came out of it. Nita bent over it and it purred. She stroked it and picked it up by the neck. So now, she had a companion. It was always better to share one *roti* bread with a friend than to have it all for oneself.

She had only taken a few steps when she realised what a fool she had been. It must be a cub she was cradling, and the mother would most likely be back soon.

'*Bou lo!*' she cried out, using the Odia word for mother. She put the cub down and ran hard towards the fire. Before she knew it, she crashed with something, took a hard tumble, and rolled on the ground. She wondered if she would stop rolling right at a tigress's mouth. A roar pierced the sounds of the jungle. In a daze, she pulled herself up and ran again.

She sensed another creature running just behind her. She turned to see a girl. The girl must have been the thing she had collided with. The lines of the girl's body were quite visible even in that faint light, and her breath was ragged. She was taller than Nita.

'Why are you after me?' Nita shouted.

'I'm – not!' the girl shouted back. 'They're after me!'

'Who?'

'He's evil. Satan himself! And his men!'

'Satan again', Nita said.

'Yes', she panted. 'That man, my uncle, he's no less than Satan. His men are after me.'

'Why?' Nita shouted between gasps.

'To kill me.'

'What?'

They were at the ring of fire. Without a word, they added some more sticks to it, and then hopped across it. The thought that it would not protect them from the men crossed her mind, but she was too tired to think too much. The girl went straight into the hole, as if it was dug out for her. Nita kept her fury to herself, and sat down on the platform. It was nice there as well. It might even have been romantic, with better company and at a better time.

'My uncle – his name is Savyasachi Chaudhuri', the girl said after a minute of quiet.

Nita had heard that name before all right. He had something of a business empire in steel, petrol and mobile phone distribution.

'The big-time businessman?' she asked.

'Yes, him. My papa and Savyasachi *chacha* – father's younger brother – are partners. *Chacha* wants me out of the way, so that papa doesn't have an heir. He got his guys to kidnap me and they were about to cut me up and throw me in this jungle where no one would have found me. I was lucky to run away from them… Listen, let's put this fire out. It'll only draw those men here.'

'Without it we'll be dinner for the tigress I was running from. And for her cub, maybe.'

The girl chuckled, but became grave very soon.

'What about those men? If they find me, they'll just...' She trailed off.

'I never signed up to be your bodyguard!' Nita said. The words just slipped out before she could control herself. She was getting angrier by the minute, at this spoilt princess who had taken away her bed. People like the Chaudhuris ... that's all they did. Live off others.

'And what did you come here for? Adventure?' The girl asked.

'Yes, I'm Sherlock Holmes's granddaughter. Well, I actually came for a picnic.'

The girl seemed to recognise that her host wasn't too happy. She kept a sullen silence for some time.

'Do you have something to eat?' she asked, in a plaintive tone this time.

This was too much. Her own hunger was driving Nita crazy.

'I have air. Want it?' She snapped.

'Do you at least have mineral water? I'm very thirsty', the girl said.

'No!' Nita shouted. 'I'm not your father's servant. I wish – God packs me off here of all places, and then you steal my hole and enjoy the fire. And then ... then you want me to rustle up dinner!'

The girl started crying.

'My father died last year. If he was still around, I wouldn't have been here.'

A stone had hurt Nita's butt while she shifted around.

'Why don't you go to your mother then?' she burst out. 'Open a five-star hotel here, enjoy life?'

'She's not alive', the girl said morosely. 'I don't have anyone. When those guys were taking me to the jungle, I wondered why God had left me. I figured it must be because of the wrong things my family did. I know they did some terrible things. Papa and his younger brother, my *chacha*, pretended to be working together, but they were really at each other's throats. I've heard that *chacha* had mummy poisoned, and papa had *chacha*'s eight-year-old son killed in retaliation. Then he lost his sleep and finally died of a heart attack. Even that didn't stop the enmity. I guess my death will.' The girl was sobbing now.

She looked so frail in the soft glow of the fire. Nita felt a pang of guilt. She was taller than Nita, but still very young. Nita reached out and squeezed her shoulder. She wanted to protect her, to be a *didi*, an elder sister. She stopped herself from wiping the girl's tears. It was better for her to let them out.

'What's in this bag?' Nita asked. The girl had clung on to a black shoulder bag all the time.

'I don't know. I picked it up when I ran, when those guys were drunk.'

It turned out to be a treasure. Salty biscuits, a bottle of water, a plain white *dhoti* – a sheet of cloth – a knife and a brand-new spade. Nita usually liked her biscuits sweet, but she wasn't complaining. By the time they had had their fill, they were a changed couple.

The girl's name was Nita as well. Nita Chaudhuri.

What next? As they talked, they concluded the men must know the girl had escaped. When they set out to capture her, they would naturally come towards the fire. They could show up at any time.

Nita told the girl about her grandmother's tale, and they started work on enacting it. She opened out her long tresses, and wore the white dhoti like a sari. She put her make-up kit to good use, making a striking red *bindi* – a big dot – on her forehead. She lined her eyes a thick black, and used white paint to give herself two small fake tusks like Satan. The girl's wide-eyed, admiring look told her she was doing okay. She told herself that if she had to leave the hill, she must carry a few embers with her, even in her bag.

She saw movement in the bush at the end of the forest. It must be the *chacha*'s men. She told the girl to stay in the hole, and she stepped out herself. She stayed near the fire. She did not have lines, but she would improvise. She felt much better than she had in a long time.

The men walked up to her. One look at them and she knew they were completely disoriented by the weird sight of the witch in the circle of fire.

'Hey there, you hag! What are you doing here?' one of them asked.

'Did you see a girl? In a white salwar suit?'

'You better talk, or I'll split your head open.' That one was the most fearsome looking, and he carried a hatchet. But his hands were trembling.

He made her angry, and helped her to lose her fear. She was on familiar ground now. She struck up a dance pose, and smiled.

'Come on, bastards. Come. I've been blood thirsty for a long time. Come to me.'

She danced with abandon now. She was in her element. The whites of her eyes showed as she rolled her eyes back. She moved her hands in graceful curves, beckoning the villains. Her grandmother had been quite graphic in her narration. So, she hoped, had theirs. It was not easy, performing in front of those three louts, when she compared it to a show in front of a thousand ticket-buying people. Her heart thudded as loudly has her bare heels did. She wondered if her new friend could hear her heartbeat. But she began to lose herself in the act.

'Come to me, come to mother', she chanted.

The one with the hatchet caved in first.

'She's a bloody witch!' He said as he turned. His haunches heaved and he kicked up dust as he sprinted away. He only looked back once. The other two stood undecided, trembling.

Nita was trembling as well, but it only helped to enhance her performance. She was laughing with relief now, moaning loudly:

'I am thirsty, give me blood, hungry, give me flesh!' It seemed to be working.

And then it went wrong.

'Look, there's my bag!' One of the two men shouted. Nita cursed herself.

'It's an act', the other one said, slowly. The two of them looked for the third man. There was no sign of him. They moved forward. Nita picked up a big burning stick, and ran with the frantic, clumsy steps of one whose life is at stake. Her instinct guided her towards the place where she had left the cub. Once the contours of the place looked familiar, she picked up stones and threw them, one by one, in as many possible directions as she could. One of them apparently hit the right spot. A ferocious snarl issued from very close. She still had the burning stick in her hand. She ran back towards the fire, taking a small arc to avoid the two men.

When the two men got there, the tigress was waiting for them, all primed up.

Nita almost collapsed when she stepped back into the circle of fire. Her feet were numb, and she felt a sharp, piercing pain at the junction of her ribs and stomach, and her heart was pounding. The roar of the tigress and the screams of the two villains told her that her plan had worked this time.

Nita junior came out of the hole, clung to her and held her tight. They stayed together for a long time without exchanging a word. After a while, Nita sank to the warm ground and lay there, watching the starlit sky. She had never seen so many stars. She soaked in the warmth of the fire, and enjoyed the feeling of having pulled off the unimaginable. God must have won the game this time.

A red tint seeped into the inky black sky, and soon the night had vanished. When they walked towards the city, their eyes had a different look about them. This time, they would not let an Arjun Mahapatra or a Savyasachi Chaudhuri trample them.

Vandana Shukla

 *SIT SLUMPED ON THE ROLLING CHAIR, and look wide-eyed at the group of people who stand around, gawking at me. They frown, pucker their lips, knit their eyebrows. At intervals, some of them place stethoscopes on different parts of my body, and seem to assess the possibilities that are embedded in the patterns of my breath. If there are any patterns. They seem to be more obsessed with my heartbeat that the state of my heart. They want to get to the bottom of the question of whether I exist. I think I am dead. Or am I? I do not believe any more that heartbeats are the primary indicator of a human's being. In principle, anything is possible. It is possible that tomorrow morning's newspaper headlines scream about my departure from the world of the living. Or that I am the star of TV news: Mr such and such, known for his art films, winner of national and international awards, passed away at the young age of… I'm not sure if the air is*

thick with rumours about the riddle of my passing away. The powers that be are conducting an enquiry into the nature and causes of my death. Was there a technical glitch? But what is this strange line of thought? In any case, I have this sinking feeling that I am an unfortunate being, like a cursed bird banished from both earth and sky, doomed to eke out a transient life somewhere in between – while people of the earth, thinking that the bird chirps happily in the sky, write their cheesy poems about its song. Sometimes I wonder if I am deranged, unhinged. In any case, in my humble opinion there is no big difference between being deranged and dead. In both situations, we commemorate our lives with our past.

A few days ago…

When I got off the plane at JFK Airport, my bones were aching, and a series of unusual videos streamed before my eyes. I found it mysterious that the atmosphere inside the plane was all about worldly desires, charged with such positive energy, but the moment I stepped out into the vast open expanses of nature I felt either blank and despondent, or supremely blissful from the bottom of my heart. I looked at the clouds swimming in the infinite sky like shapeless cotton balls, and when I saw this relationship of detachment between sky and cloud, I felt an inner peace, as if my soul had found a home. I smiled as I thought about it, and thought, as I smiled, about the silent dialogue between my soul and that scene. What was it about? Was it an agreement that my soul would be back, be among those clouds as one of them – except that the time wasn't defined and my body was not to know about it. I smiled again.

Noise had reigned throughout the flight. It was different from the usual noise, though, the type that can be boring to the point of cruelty. I dreamed on in a pleasant half-sleep. I guess I looked like I was slumbering. The girl in the seat behind me broke into loud peals of laughter every now and then. She might have thought I was fast asleep, or maybe she did not care. My other neighbours were busy pestering the stewardess for drinks. I was at peace – I had no complaints. When I set foot outside the airport, a gentle cold had dissolved into the twilight. A little earlier, I had picked up my suitcase off the belt, and afterwards, I had adjusted my hat, tightened my belt a notch – I had loosened it in the flight – and tugged on my tie to check that it was all right. I felt like a smoke, but I wanted to reach the hotel first. I fished out the card from my coat in a reflex action – I had already seen and fingered it many times, but there was something reassuring about the touch and sight of it. I only had to crane my neck for a second or two before I found what I was looking for. In the crowd of people waiting for travellers, there was a middle-aged white man holding a board that proclaimed 'The Great Pandora Hotel'. His eyes lit up, as I am sure mine did, and I thanked God for sparing me the trouble of expending labour to trace out my host.

'Welcome, Sir!' He said. 'I am Freddie.' An identity card dangled from his neck, which certified he was who he claimed to be.

I smiled back at him.

'Please follow me', he said, as he took my suitcase and led me up an escalator. 'And how was your journey, sir?' He asked when our relative positions permitted it, with his head bent at a solicitous angle.

I knew that my first impression had not been wrong. He exuded politeness. We continued to chat until we reached the point where the river of passengers flows into the mouth of the airport, and from where the forces of the city escort them to their destinations.

The clean, wide streets glistened in the lights. It must have rained; the streets looked like they had been wiped clean. They were lined by trees with big, bright, yellowing leaves that seemed to move to an irregular but continuous beat. It was a comforting, noiseless drive in the red limousine. The international conference in Chicago was about advances in film and entertainment technology. I was one of the invitees. We were mostly quiet in the car, probably because of a mix of exhaustion and inhibition.

We were climbing a sloping bridge, and then the road levelled in front of the imposing hotel. To our right, there was a huge, manicured garden and a swimming pool surrounded by grey stone towers that had glass walls on the ground floor. The hotel was bathed in a light that made it look serene. A wide group of reception desks showed some signs of activity. They were managed by smartly turned out hotel staff with what seemed to be very natural smiles. There was a water tank filled with beautiful red and white lilies, and the floors of the tank displayed an iridescent mix of refracted colours through its clear blue water. I wondered if the strains of music that wafted in the air were coming from through the water. At the counter, I met five other conference-attendees, all of us from different countries. Freddie was still with us, and working his way with consummate ease through the required formalities of checking in.

We were being taken to our rooms. The lift stopped at the thirty-sixth floor, and we stepped out onto a plush carpet. An endless, wide corridor was lined with paintings that showed off the city's landmarks or had period advertisements featuring svelte women with bobbed and curled hair from the 1920s. A hint of a scent I could not identify – perhaps it was lavender – and the soothing music made me feel slightly numb. Room 103 was allotted to me, and the two adjoining rooms were given to two of the others, Howard and Kim. Howard was American, a journalist and screenwriter from California. Kim was South Korean, and owned a gaming software company. As for me, Suryakant Prabhakar 'Shalabh' (that last one was an adopted name), I was a writer, art film maker and theatre director. Freddie had facilitated our introductions. We hit it off quite well. There must have been more to it than our being neighbours and in our forties. I guess, as always, it helped to have overlapping viewpoints.

It was night, and we were drinking in the balcony as the lights of the golden city twinkled in the distance. There is something different about tippling with strangers from other countries. You do not know much about the others, and you do not want to. We kept the conversation light. Howard, for example, had just divorced his wife of three years over differences of opinion, but they planned to stay good friends. Kim had three kids, and his wife was a receptionist because she wanted an income of her own. As for me… I was single. I sensed their surprise, but as I had expected, they covered up well, and soon we moved beyond the matter of personal particulars.

Up there on the thirty-sixth floor, it was a particularly starry view. Through the spotless glass, the traffic on the snaking roads gave an impression of canals of golden light. Howard had a cigar sticking out of his mouth, like in a western. Howard had much to say about the 9/11 attacks, and his eyes became animated as if he was reliving that fateful day. He talked about how he had seen buildings of concrete and steel collapse like a house of cards, and how he had overcome his guilt to capture some of the sights in his camera. Kim listened more than he talked, but the few words that he spoke on gaming and animation were enough to convey his deep understanding of the topic.

Howard changed the topic several times, first talking of roulette. He said he loved it. He said he wanted to live the Nazi years in Germany, just to understand how those abhorred years felt. He had heard Ravi Shankar play the guitar. He still remembered the magic touch of the maestro's blurring fingers on the strings. The discussion meandered to the opera and classical Greek theatre.

Kim was puffing on a cigarette, and sipping vodka in between. He said:

'Actually, our eyes are like cameras. Scenes stay stored in them, and they can even be saved. All that's needed is to make sure we get the scenes transferred to canvas or paper before loading other scenes.' He took a puff and exhaled smoke politely, so that it didn't impinge on either of us. 'Memory – now that's a bloody unreliable faculty. Memories are completely fickle.'

I am not very sure, but that was probably the last line of the night. Our drinks were done, and we were ready to crash.

⁂

At the breakfast table, Kim and I shared a few anecdotes, and then we got talking about the new toy that was about to be unveiled, Dreamland. I confessed I was crazy to experience it. It was beyond my understanding. Howard joined us then.

'To my mind', I said, 'the science fiction film takes you through a tunnel of philosophy and spirituality to a destination of determinism.'

'That's because we are basically discoverers by nature', Howard responded. 'Our curiosity takes us beyond the Earth, Solar System and Milky Way to the whole of the Cosmos. That's the driving force behind the genre. And while I'm not a hardcore theist, I do believe that every discovery, in the end, is rooted in the search for an eternal truth.'

The next days were full of similar discussions, and the conference's scheduled presentations kept us busy.

On the morning of the fourth day. The silver art deco-style clock in the hotel room woke me up at six thirty, as effectively as someone pounding on the door.

'Good morning, ladies and gentlemen, it is six thirty, and time to rise.' One more time, the pleasant feminine tone of the morning call spread through the room like a perfume.

The wall in front of me became a screen, and the projection of a beautiful dark girl appeared on it. With a bright smile, she announced,

'Hello, dear guest. For this evening, after the closing presentations, the main attraction is Dreamworld, the new gizmo. And you and your fellow guests have the honour of inaugurating it!' She seemed quite pleased with that, I thought, and she faded away looking happy.

During the conference sessions, we had learned a bit about the tech behind the game, and its functionalities. Of course, time travel in films was old hat, but it seemed this would be different. It would be more experiential, they told us with meaningful looks. When we met, Howard, Kim and I were all set to make the journey.

It was night when we stepped into a large oval laboratory and made our way to a giant, chrome rocking chair with about a dozen seats in it. As I strapped myself to my seat, I saw Kim exulting like a teenager. He gave me the 'yo' sign, and I returned it. There were screens in front of our seats. As the lights went out, a helmet descended in front of me, and I followed the instructions on the screen to fasten it. It seemed to have been made for me. I had looked forward to this H.G. Wells-Jules Verne experience for days. Now that I was living it, I already felt like I was in a dream. A bald man in a simple white robe appeared on the screen and greeted us with a bow.

'Good evening, *namaste* and *anyoung haseyo*', he said in a slightly robotic tone. 'This experiential journey will last for nine hours and forty-five minutes. So physically you will be here until the morning. You will first select your preferences by visually choosing the options on the forms that will appear on this screen next. For example, you can choose whether you would like a male or female narrator for your journey, which parts of history you are interested in, and so on. You cannot change your preferences once the journey starts.' The man morphed into a dark shape and then disappeared.

I felt like the early astronauts who went out to places where no man had gone before. I felt a sudden urge to abandon my atheism. A part of me was scared about what would happen if the game failed, trapping me in time like the Connecticut Yankee. I had so much unfinished strings to tie up – there was a project in post-production, in addition to a couple of pending shoots.

I craned my neck to check out the other two. Our visors were clear, and those guys looked extremely scared. I fought back the impulse to get out of the seat and run for the door. It helped that it was dark, I was belted, and I had forgotten where the door was.

I chose a female narrator.

The screen had a question for me. 'What do you want to see?'

I spoke into the microphone. 'The period of the Second World War.'

'Got it', was the message in response. The screen flashed images of the D-Day landings, the fall of Singapore, Dunkirk, the taking of Iwo Jima and a mushroom cloud. In a few seconds, I felt a thud a bit like when the plane tyres hit the tarmac.

The darkness lifted in an instant, and I found myself in a room. I looked around, and figured it was the front deck of a ship. There were a lot of mirrors, and I was standing on a polished wooden floor. Right in front of me, wearing a shimmering dark-blue gown, and smiling a very poised smile, stood a beautiful brunette. 'Welcome aboard, sir. Which country are you from?'

'India', I said. I felt that I might have been too curt, but I was rather disoriented by the sudden lights, the change in scene and the pretty girl.

'Shall we talk in Hindi, then, unless you speak another language?' she said.

'Hindi is fine', I said, taken aback.

'*Kyaa lenge aap*, what would you like to drink? I know Indians like masala chai and filter coffee. Am I wrong?' I loved the way she spoke. She seemed to take a genuine pleasure in her ability to serve me. Her smile was dazzling.

'You're absolutely right, madam', I said, using the honorific *aap* to address her.

'Oh please call me Joyce', she said. 'And please use *tum*', she added. That is the most familiar form of address in Hindi.

'Thank you', I said, 'it's a nice name.'

'So, you're interested in history?' She asked. Her smile was enchanting, and I realised what it was about her that made me look so deep into her eyes that I almost felt embarrassed. It was her dimples.

'Yes, you could say that. I'm mainly into directing film and theatre, and I'm greatly inspired by some foreign writers.'

'No doubt. We know about you, of course', she said. The smile flitted over her face, and after that, never left it for long. She conveyed a sense of encouraging and supporting everything I said, even the most trivial thing, while also taking it very seriously. She had an incredible ability to bond.

In some moments, I turned loquacious. I needed an interesting topic and good company. I had never heard it said by anyone else – it was just a conclusion I have reached on my own. This was one of those moments.

'I would like to experience the Second World War the way the writers of that age experienced it.'

She listened in that way that she had, and it egged me on.

'There's no special difference between the situation then and now', I said. 'Some analysts say there is a difference, that in those times there were exogenous variables that created troubles and now it's controlled actions that create them. We don't have an all-out war, perhaps, but we are still watching the conflict between those who have power and those who want more unfold before us. And this conflict swallows societies and countries. It's probably no exaggeration to say that it has engulfed most parts of the world.'

I am not sure, but I think Dreamworld worked so well that I forgot I was in a simulated world. I acted as naturally as if I was unwinding in an Irani cafe in Mumbai. On the other hand, I also felt a nagging irritation at how our past had clung to our existence.

She interlocked her fingers that were sheathed in silky gloves, and a curled lock of her hair fell on her forehead.

'You're right', she said. 'I think it's a mistaken notion that human nature and actions are a function of time and space. They aren't that foreign – I think they're quite innate.'

There was a lull in our conversation. In that spacious room, with just the two of us, we could hear the sounds of the waves lapping against the hull of the ship.

'It's ironic that so much loved literature and film come out of a period of so much strife, death and misery', she said. The sea breeze was mist and cool. A flight of sea gulls made a noisy landing on the waves. 'So, which writer's experiences do you want to live?' Joyce asked me.

'It's up to you', I said. 'You drive.' The words slipped out – they were not really shaped before I mouthed them. I thought she would find it a strange idea, and perhaps reject it, but she responded her usual way. She smiled a gracious smile, as if I had made a very useful suggestion.

There were still some noisy seagulls around. A couple of them had parked on the railing, their wings glowing in the soft evening light. The sky was a mix of grey and saffron. The cold was palpable, but it was just at the right intensity level to be bracing without making me uncomfortable. The lights came on inside, and the play of light on Joyce's face had me enthralled. For some time, she turned to gaze at the gentle rise and fall of the waves, while I admired her.

I felt a jolt, something like being woken up by the realisation that it was way too bright and the alarm had failed to buzz. It was a little like being between two sleeps. It took me a while to figure out what had happened. I had entered a different world, one in which we were on land; on an uneven, narrow, long muddy road that was obviously much travelled on. I could discern a row of bent, ageing trees that seemed to be lazing in the dim light. Behind them, there were small houses with no space between them. A few of them were two-storied. They had small, ancient-looking green wooden windows. A few of the inhabitants had shut out the outside with thick curtains. On the road with us, there was a crowd of men and women, in long dresses, and trudging along under unevenly shaped loads.

'We are in World War II France. This is the road to Goderville, and these are farmers from Normandy.' We reached a fork in the road. On our right, we saw a cafe where a few people sat on wooden benches. Their clothes suggested that they were not very wealthy. A few ducks strutted and squawked near them. There was a barnyard that had a couple of carts and other paraphernalia of village life.

We followed the crowd and turned into another dirt road. The smell of stables, animals, dung and hay filled the air. The road was lined by trees that were leafy on their upper sides but sparse below. A few horsemen came galloping down the road as if they owned it. They wore long hats, loose trousers, and dark overcoats. No doubt, they were German officers.

I was shoved from behind as someone pushed me. I had stopped suddenly. What were cavalrymen doing in World War II? I looked at Joyce and she nodded as we walked on, as if to comfort me.

'You see, Dreamworld is still a beta version. It can mix up a few timelines. In any case, how sure are we about timelines anyway?'

I pondered that as we shuffled through the crowd.

In the throng, there were a few carriages that transported women who sat ramrod straight and looked through the crowd as they smiled and talked to each other. I guess they were the officers' wives. It took me a while to figure out what was odd about the carriages. They were drawn by groups of five or six barely dressed men with their ribs and shoulder blades showing. There were also men in black shirts swaggering down the road, carrying rifles and bearing shiny medals on their chests. The thumping of their heavy boots seemed to create a tension in the air.

Joyce and I walked hurriedly, with bags strapped to our backs. She wore a brown dress that covered her slim, toned body from neck to toe. A dark scarf covered her head and most of her face. We turned onto a more even path that was slightly less crowded.

Joyce was closer to me now. I luxuriated in the warmth of her closeness, even though she was sheathed in the most unromantic dress. I loved the tingling touch of her gloveless fingers on my wrist. She whispered into my ear,

'We are close to Château de Miromesnil. The houses that you see are of Norman farmers, who live in very oppressed conditions.' Joyce went silent for a while, as if she had a lump in her throat.

It was an emotional moment for me. I was all right with the time being jumbled up; this was the holy intersection of time and space that I had wanted to walk, in an impossible dream. And here I was, in France, in a hazy period from the last century, and who knows who had walked this earth that I was leaving my footprints on? Maupassant, Flaubert, Voltaire! And why should they only be French? Perhaps Gorky was here, and Imre Kertész? I felt a pleasure that was beyond anything I had experienced, and Joyce's electrifying presence heightened it. A tiny, recalcitrant grey cell reminded me that it was a dream, and my heart said that if it was, may it last for ever.

The sky was darkening. We now walked past a dense forest with monstrous, twisted trees. Their roots were like a giant ascetic's untended beard. Fireflies shimmered in the light of dusk. I imagined elves dancing in the dark of the forest. I could almost hear the patter of their tiny feet on the soft earth. It felt as if the forest was inviting us inside. I drew Joyce close to me, and walked faster until we had left it behind us.

We could see the lights of a town. We were approaching a building that had a huge doorway with a triangular section.

'Are we in Maupassant's town?' I asked Joyce.

My happiness shone in her eyes.

'That's right', she said. 'I'm glad you recognised it. It made my bringing you here worth it. We have come here through the Dieppe area, a part of France whose extreme conditions and contradictions Maupassant had seen from very close quarters. His family was broken, and he didn't know much about discipline and etiquette. He could jump into the river to swim when he liked, and he'd stay in there for hours. He was, of course, a great patroniser of prostitutes.' She sighed, and for a long while we only heard our footsteps.

We walked in through the doorway, past some sculptures on the side walls and entered a large, circular theatre. Some people lounged on stone benches. It was a floating crowd, with people trickling in and leaving as time passed. Most of the crowd were men in blue coats and hats who stood out with their ridiculous erect postures. The theatre echoed with the thuds of their heels. Some of them had their arms around the waists of their women companions. Some women who were on their own, and others who were with other women, sat in the front rows, and they were better dressed. They were probably wives of the German officers. We sat down on an empty stone bench, and waited for the show to start. Before I knew it, Joyce's hand was in mine. I'm not sure if I was scared that in that dim light someone would come between us.

Without warning, the theatre blacked out. I waited for the lights to focus on stage, but before that I felt a comforting heaviness descend on me like a heavy blanket.

The hall full of people faded into darkness. It felt as if the blackness of many winter nights had been distilled into the pitch darkness of the theatre. I felt a rumble in my buttocks and soles, and I realised that I had transformed from a viewer to an actor in the play. I was riding a carriage. The stage was not a wooden one any more; it was a long road lined with a row of gas lamps that put out feeble and foggy glow. We were approaching an unlit part of the road that had thick trees around it.

I knew that my facial features had changed – the patterns of my breath, the way I saw things, the feel of my lips, everything was different except for my torso… but who knew, perhaps that had changed as well. I wore a thick frock coat and pantaloons that became tight on my legs near my heavy, shiny boots. I was a big man, travelling without a companion. I held a big walking stick with a lion-shaped brass head. There were a few couples whose clothes and expressions had an expensive lustre about them. It crossed my mind that I had seen them somewhere. Was it in something I had read? A faint memory almost came to me, but it flitted away leaving just a hint – it had something to do with my turning a page, and having moist eyes long ago. No, wait, I realised it was in a theatre where I had been waiting for a play to start.

Two nuns sat in a corner, looking identical – scared and worried. Rosaries were tied to their waistbands. Right in front of me was a woman you could not take your eyes off. I knew her, and so did all of France. Elisabeth Rousset, the prostitute. I knew her through the pages of a book, pages that

I had thumbed hundreds of times. She wore an attractive pink dress and a matching hat. A veil covered her eyes, but it only enhanced their brilliance. Those eyes, and the curve of her generous lips, told the world that she knew the effect she had on others.

I just could not remove my eyes from hers. I willed myself to look away, but I could not move any further than her lips. What if I tried to find an actress to play her part, in another life? No, it was not possible. She looked out of the window and released me from her grip, with a faint smile. I almost felt a pain in my heart when I realised that her smile was not reflected in those eyes that – just for a second – showed a glimpse of deep grief. I looked at the other women in the carriage, and saw how they sneered at her, with all their energy and focus. Would Joyce have done that? Where was Joyce? I missed the touch of her hand.

I looked again at the beautiful woman in front of me, and at that moment, I realised Joyce would grow, about ten years later, to look exactly like her. The bells of a church pealed somewhere in the distance.

The coachman had stopped for a while. He stood outside, smoking and sharing jokes with a couple of other men. Before they started, he drew the curtains and lit the two lamps inside the carriage, bathing it in a warm yellow light that highlighted Elisabeth Rousset's beauty in a different kind of way.

We were fleeing the war front, trying to escape to a place relatively safe from the marauding

Prussians. The carriage hurtled through the dark, taking them closer to safety each minute.

A guttural shout rang out, and the carriage lurched to a halt. One of the horses whinnied. A pair of curtains was pulled apart, and we saw a stiff Prussian officer on horseback blocking the road. It was incredible – we had strayed into Prussian Territory. He got off the horse and strode towards the carriage door. I am not ashamed to say that each ring of his boots made us cringe in fear. The coachman opened the door for him, and he looked at each of the passengers with his cold grey eyes, one foot on the stepladder, hand resting on his thigh.

'Get the carriage off the road', he ordered the cowed coachman. 'You're not going anywhere. Unless the woman here joins me for the night.'

We knew the woman he had in mind was Elisabeth. She was looking outside the window dreamily, and she did not react. It was almost as if she knew that this would pass.

The officer's lips curled, and he stroked his moustache. 'What's it going to be?' he said to no one in particular, and turned away, ignoring the incoherent pleas of the other passengers.

They set to work at once on Elisabeth, and I watched silently, as time passed. Every minute brought us closer to a cruel fate. I knew that Elisabeth would never give herself to Prussians. The women who had been sneering at Elisabeth earlier were the most cogent in their rationalisations of why Elisabeth should give in. In tones that they would use for their equals and superiors, they explained that the consequences of rejection could be worse – she may have to submit to many Prussians instead of only the one. They mentioned their children, and how they wished to see them before death, or a worse, fate fell upon them.

I wanted to say 'Stop this, let her be!' I said nothing. I looked on as the horror unfolded before me.

During a lull in the entreaties from the women, Elisabeth got up, and stepped out of the carriage. She followed the officer, taking two steps for each of his. He lifted her up onto his horse and rode away.

The women, and their husbands, were chattering away now. I did not take advantage of the openings they gave me to join the discussion. They speculated on whether 'that woman' could come back at all. What if she ran away? What if the Prussian did not keep his word? What were the chances that he would? Oh, how hungry and thirsty they were, and they had carried so little with them, it would hardly last that long night. And time, oh time, that greatest of traitors, how slowly it trickled!

Dawn was breaking when I heard the door shut. It was Elisabeth. She sat in her old place, without a word. It was too dark for me to see her clearly. I wondered how she would react if I reached out and patted her hand. I did nothing.

The carriage rumbled off, and it felt as if we were driving towards sunshine. The coachman flogged the horses and we exulted in the speed with which we raced towards happiness. I looked at Elisabeth with a heavy heart. In the light of the day, I saw her struggle to raise her eyes. When she did look up, she looked at one of the women with a new light in her eyes, some hope, a little like the look that a child would offer when she knows that she has done something difficult for the first time. One by one, the women ignored her with a final brutality that made me shudder. It was as if we had returned to the day before. Nothing had changed.

When she looked at me, I am ashamed to say, she turned away immediately, but not before her eyes had flickered in despair. Our eyes never met again.

That glimmer in her eyes, and the moments that led to it stubbornly resisted all my efforts to erase it from my memory. On the other hand, another part of me wanted to study it again and again as a sequence of scenes. I even liked reliving the entangled joy and pain of the carriage ride. Was it because I had a sadistic bent? Was it originally an innate cruel streak that surfaced in me? I felt a bit unwell as I pondered all this. We had arrived. The others alighted without a word to those they had not been conversing with. I got down first and offered Elisabeth my hand, ignoring the contemptuous looks the women gave me. She did not take my hand. I could not see her eyes through the veil. My eyes were moist.

'Joyce!' I called out as she walked past me. She did not falter for a few steps, and then she turned around, drew her veil and looked at me. 'Joyce, are you all right?'

'Yes. A little tired', she said.

I had to strain to hear her. Her lips had lost their confident smile and her face, its sheen. What was left was a haggard, jaded beauty that made me want to kiss her gently on her forehead. I saw a bead of sweat on her forehead, like a drop of dew on a rose. She turned and started walking. I followed her.

'Where are you going?' I asked. 'I… I want to—' I winced in pain as a strong light blinded me, blacking out my vision completely. I sat collapsed in a chair. When I could see again, all I saw was a blank screen without a reflection.

A familiar, unwanted, face formed on the screen. It was the bald man in the white robe.

'Welcome back', he said with a satisfied smile. 'How was your journey, gentlemen?'

My throat was parched and my arms and legs felt like they were made of lead.

'Where is Joyce?' I asked.

The man did not seem to make an effort to change his smile, but I thought it had suddenly turned into a very nasty one.

I gulped and fought back my tears. I hated my effeminate sound.

'Please, can I see her right now?'

The man grinned, and his cheeks crinkled.

'I'm afraid not, sir. That feature is still in development. It will be a few years before it is available in our product line.'

The lab was full of men in suits. They were exulting, slapping each other's backs, talking loudly, flushed with their success.

All I wanted was to tell Joyce that I could not live without her.

Professor 800

Dileep Shakya

HE LAWNS OF HOTEL TAJ MANSINGH were buzzing. Fatima Bhutto, the big name Pakistani writer was releasing her latest work, *Sons of the Blood and Sword*. William Dalrymple, champagne glass in hand, talked to her in his familiar style. The cameras flashed. The November night had descended, and the lights of the bar beckoned. Some of the glitterati engaged the writer in conversation. Others headed for the bar.

Professor 800 was expounding on the exquisite taste of Chivas Regal to a friend, who was also a writer, although not as well-known as Bhutto. The professor looked at her watch. It was eleven.

'It's time to go, darling', she said. 'My parents are returning tomorrow morning.'

The professor and her writer friend gathered their handbags and moved towards the lifts, stopping to shake hands on the way. The lift was fashionable – it had mirrors on all four walls. Even more striking was the lift attendant, a shapely figure dressed in a shimmering pink georgette sari. She spoke softly, with polish, as she escorted the two ladies to their car.

The writer asked her driver to turn FM on. It was Neelesh Mishra's programme, 'Memories of the City', belting out a Bollywood oldie.

'This guy is a favourite of mine', the writer said. 'He's got style. And what a voice. Husky…'

The professor cut her short. 'Tell me, is there anything to this book of Bhutto's?'

'Nothing, baby, nothing', the writer slurred. 'It's all show off… big money, big family. All drama, no substance.'

'Yah, that's what I think. It's all feudal anyway, isn't it? Sword, blood, song – everything. I think there was one great writer in Pakistan, pure anti-feudal. Faiz Ahmad Faiz. Aah, the others pale in comparison.' She hummed a couple of lines from Faiz, and the writer joined her: 'When the thrones are upturned, the crowns are tossed away, we shall see… we shall see.'

The car zipped down the deserted streets of Delhi, past traffic lights – which the denizens of the city call red lights in spite of their evident multicoloured capabilities – and roundabouts. They would have continued to enjoy the heady mix of oldies on FM, their reminiscences of Faiz and the night breeze, but the professor said, 'My place. Tell him to turn left.'

The university gate loomed almost as soon as the driver turned the steering hard. The professor called her mother as soon as they stepped into the flat. It turned out that her parent's train had just crossed Bhopal.

Professor 800 was a nickname her students gave her. She had found it rather cheap at first, but then, had got used to it. She was Head of the Department of Comparative Literature at the university. Three years before, her parents had died in a train crash. After their deaths, Professor 800 became a recluse. She was past forty, and still single in spite of having many apparently attractive proposals. She lived comfortably in the faculty staff quarters. She had this feeling that marriage would distance her from her friends and parents. Before the train crash ended her life, her mother had tried to talk her out of this insecurity, and failed.

Her mother had been a big-time fiction writer until a few years ago. Her father was a manager in a public sector bank, and he had just retired a few days before the crash. After having worked in about half the big cities in India, he wanted to live out the rest of his life in the same city as his daughter. Her parents were relocating from Hyderabad to Delhi when the train crashed.

It was a pleasantly cold night in November, at about three in the morning. A bomb went off in the train just before it crossed Dholpur. The professor was in her class the next day. A friend who had gone to receive her parents texted her:

'Bomb blast in the coach. No one alive. I think we have lost them. Come immly.'

She felt the floor wobble.

'No, this can't happen!' She said to herself, but then she realised the whole class was stunned into silence. No one moved or spoke for a long time. Then a blurred, earnest face entered her field of vision and asked,

'Is everything all right, ma'am?'

She said, 'No. I'm not well. I have to go.' The next thing she knew, she was in the car and speeding towards the station.

~•°○◡○°•~

That was three years ago. Sometimes, she still saw a speeding train exploding in a ball of flames in the frame of the blackboard. The thought of her parents' bodies being atomised made her feel faint.

She had become a completely different person, and it started to show in her work in strange ways. Her febrile mind had become twice as creative. She changed the way she taught. The anecdotes she told about writers did not exist in any known records. In her references to novels and stories, the plots got twisted and characters invented. She shared fabricated insights with her students – and they suffered for believing her.

The last semester's results had been such a disaster that her students complained en masse to the Vice Chancellor. The Vice Chancellor set up a secret enquiry committee. As usual, the committee did not stay secret for long. The professor heard about it, and became even more unhinged. Now she saw detectives shadowing her wherever she went – at home, on the road, in lifts, in the class.

The Department of Comparative Literature was housed in a brand-new building. It was not fully occupied. The professor liked the echoing emptiness of its corridors.

She had a class to teach on the eleventh floor. She enjoyed the ringing of her footsteps in the quiet of the afternoon. She stepped into the lift with her phone in hand. She had this habit of sending out text messages whenever she got into a lift. Her friends would often ask which lift she was texting from. She started tapping on her phone with practised ease as she pressed the close button. She stopped after a few strokes. She had this feeling that she was on camera. She looked around her carefully, searching for the hidden eye. For a moment, she sensed that someone had stopped the lift. Her armpits were damp with sweat. She forced herself to take slower and deeper breaths. The three sides of the lift had mirrors. For an instant, she thought she saw blurred strangers standing in between her infinite reflections. Holding the rail to steady herself, she clicked a few pictures and sent them to the writer. She asked the writer to meet her at the restaurant.

This was no ordinary restaurant. It was in one of the busiest parts of the city, but it was hard to get to. There was this street that was called the Street of Bangles. With the liberalisation of the nineties, the street had taken on a new character. While some shops still clung on to their dowdy past, most had switched to selling modern beauty products. The street was now patronised by the women of the ever-expanding nouveau riche.

In between the bangle shops that jostled each other, a narrow door seemed to announce the presence of a home. The door was inconspicuous except for the Madhubani-style paintings that adorned it. A closer look at the paintings would show that there were no men in them – there were only women, children, animals and birds. Next to the door, near its top right corner, was a pink oblong plate that announced in white letters: 'M-800. Only for ladies.' The professor liked the resemblance to her nickname.

It was seven in the evening. The professor and the writer sat at one of the tables in M-800, looking worried. They nursed their half-empty glasses of Absolut. The professor brushed back the curls of hair that had strayed on to her cheeks. She said, 'Now look at this restaurant. Does it have a place in our society? Everything is managed by women – and look how well things work. But I'm not sure people will acknowledge it. We're sitting here in the flesh, right? We're not imagining this? Or are we?'

'Well, yes, we're here all right, and it works beautifully, this place. But let's not get off-track. Let's talk about your problem.'

'My problem, hmm. I'm a problem, darling. My Vice Chancellor has set up a secret enquiry against me. Everyone in the university knows that I'm a psycho: I'm not teaching literature anymore, I'm teaching imagination. On the other hand, what's literature without imagination? You tell me, you're the writer. Why do we call you a writer of fiction, and not a writer of reality?'

'Well, that's okay, baby, but the classroom isn't the right place to exercise these theories, I think.'

'No, no – I think the classroom is exactly the place. The class is a teacher's lab. That's where a teacher should experiment.'

'You mean it doesn't matter if your students fail, or you get a suspension. No, I don't think that's right.'

'Do you think I do what I do deliberately? No, it's all inbuilt in me. I'm haunted by Derrida's ghost.'

'Ha ha, Derrida. I think you need one more.' The writer spoke into a spherical webbed microphone at the centre of the table: 'One more, please.'

In almost no time, a waitress appeared, dressed in a knee-length sleeveless dress made of black and white threads. She filled their glasses.

As the professor raised the glass to her lips this time, her eyes locked on to a corner of the room and froze. Her eyebrow shot up and she stiffened.

'Hey, are you okay?' The writer asked.

'We're being watched. Let's move', the professor said.

'Come on, *yaar*, there's no one around!'

'Not anymore, but a couple of minutes ago there was. See that red table there? It had a box-like thing on it. I'm sure it was a camera. We've been recorded. She flitted in and took it away…'

'Who?'

'A woman in a long black gown and a white hat that covered her face. She wore white Bally shoes.'

The writer looked at the professor with a raised right eyebrow and a crinkled forehead.

The professor sighed.

'Don't believe me. Go ahead, call me a psycho. But I'm not lying. She was there!'

'Okay, calm down. Let me think.' The writer scratched under her chin. 'Right, let's call the waitress. Maybe you're right.' She pressed a switch on the microphone.

'What can I do for you madam?' A voice intoned.

'Bill, please.'

The waitress appeared very soon with the bill.

The writer pointed towards the red table.

'A lady was there a while back. Black gown, white hat, white shoes. Has she gone?'

'There wasn't anyone there, ma'am', the waitress said with a smile.

'I think there was', the professor interjected. 'And there was a little blue box.'

'No such thing, ma'am', the waitress's smile turned sweeter. She had dimples. She swiped the professor card and handed her the slip to sign.

'Are you sure?' The professor asked as she signed the slip without looking at it.

'Oh yes, ma'am.'

'Okay, thanks', the writer said. She signalled the professor to move.

'Thanks for the visit, ladies. Have a nice evening', the waitress said. She smiled again and bowed her head.

As soon as they were out of M-800, the professor rasped, 'She's lying. I'm sure the lady was there. I think I'm being stalked.'

'Why? What's going on? Do you have an enemy?' The writer called her driver on her mobile.

'I don't know, but I'm scared. And you probably don't believe me. Should I see a psychiatrist?'

'Well… I think you're just super stressed. You need a break. Take a long leave. No books, no classes.'

'Oh I don't think I'll need a leave. You've already predicted I'm heading for a suspension.'

'Ha-ha. Let's see if he has it in him. I guarantee you I'll write an expose on him. I'll change my name if I don't.'

'Forget that. What's in a name? I'll change mine anyway, some day. I just want to remember you as you are. I hope I don't forget you some day.'

'If you do, baby, I'll beat you till you get your memory back.'

'Comforting thought. Let's hope we never see the day.'

In their vodka-induced high, they found the buzz of the Street of Bangles a bit surreal. The professor had this feeling that she was in a dream. She made an effort to stop thinking about it. The car was waiting for them when they reached the end of the street. Good timing, he could not have waited too long. They drove through the crowded streets with the meandering streams of traffic. The writer dropped the professor home, said good night and turned homewards.

The next day, the phone rang when the professor had just settled at her desk. It was the Vice Chancellor's PA. She was to report to the Vice Chancellor at twelve sharp. She figured the countdown to her getting the boot had started. She called the PA and ordered a coffee to lighten her mood.

She knocked at the Vice Chancellor's door at exactly twelve, and she was out of his door at exactly ten past twelve. The ten minutes in between marked the end of her tenure at the university. The Vice Chancellor first praised her academic achievements in his most diplomatic persona. Then he expressed his condolences for her parents' death. Only after that did he place the students' written complaints and the recommendations of the enquiry committee in front of her.

'I say this as an elder brother, not as a Vice Chancellor: you need to get out of the world of fiction, into real life', he said. 'Loneliness is a human's biggest enemy. You can't fight it alone. That is why the family exists. That is why families form societies. I suggest you apply for a six-month leave. I am ready to sanction it without condition. Now, say what you have to say.'

'I have nothing to say, sir. I will do as you advise. Thanks for your concern. I will try to change.'

As she left the Vice Chancellor's office, the professor felt a pang of regret. She could have spoken her mind. She could have said, 'Speaking as an elder brother is fiction anyway, and by the way, the notion of loneliness as an enemy is quite fictional as well.' But maybe she had said what she should have said, for once. Still, she felt like a defeated soldier returning from a battle. She toyed with the idea of turning back, but dropped it. She knew that she had a strange tension written all over her face. She traced the lines of the tension with her fingers.

She did not want to stay in the university for another second. She walked straight to her office, filled in her leave application, organised her belongings, explained everything that needed explaining to the clerk and went straight to her trusted old Maruti 800 car without bothering to meet any of her colleagues.

Just as she released the clutch to drive off, the engine died. She started the car again, and the engine coughed to life. But it petered out as soon as she tried to drive. This went on for some time. She found she could not get a grip on the play between the clutch and the accelerator, which used to come as naturally as breathing to her. Her feet seemed to have turned to quivering jelly. Her thoughts turned to her first day on the job, when her father had gifted her this car. She could drive, of course, but in her excitement that day it had taken her a lot of effort to manage the gear changes smoothly.

It struck her that this was the very spot she had parked her car that day. How charged she had been, how full of positivity. She looked at the signboard at the entrance with a mix of anger and dejection. 'Department of Comparative Literature', it proclaimed.

The Vice Chancellor's words came back to her: Get out of the world of fiction, get real.

'Real life? Oh…' She said aloud.

It was a July afternoon. The sky had been clear, but it suddenly became overcast. Large plops of rain came down on the windshield. Or was she imagining this? She put her hand out of the open window. The pink cup of her palm filled up with water, one drop at a time. She withdrew her hand and washed her face with the rainwater. She felt a calm descend on her. When she started the car this time, the engine kept firing and she drove off. By now the rain was drumming hard on the windshield and the frantically working wipers could not keep her field of vision from turning grey. She focused her eyes beyond the wipers and used her mental map of the campus to crawl home.

She ran the few steps separating her from shelter, and picked up her mail from the letter box near the stairwell. She dropped the mail on the table without looking at it, and put together a quick lunch, a vegetarian sandwich. She stretched on the sofa with the sandwich and flicked on the TV news channels, thinking she might improve her sense of reality. Perhaps she should have been surprised; the channels were oozing their usual, fictive, imagined, tawdry bytes. Some of the channels were video versions of magazines like the famous *Manohar Kahaniyan* (Entertaining Stories) and *Satya Katha* (True Story). The most ridiculous part of it all was the crass, jarring mix of visual effects, animation and music they used for emphasis. If this was reality, what was fiction?

She switched the TV off, threw the remote to one side and picked up the letters. She put them aside one by one, until one caught her eye. The envelope was made of black plastic. The upper left corner had a sticker with her address. She flipped it over, but the sender's name was missing. The sticker had a small seal on it, which looked like that of a courier company. She peered at it, but all she could make out was that it was a combination of Xs, Ys, Zs and zeroes.

She traced the edges of the envelope, and then all of its sides, but it did not have a ridge that suggested itself as the starting place to open it. Very curious. She looked again at the sticker and started to scratch it off with her thumbnails. Success. As the shreds of the sticker came off, she could distinguish a sentence typed in very fine white letters: 'Touch your finger here.' Which finger? She chose her right index finger. When she pressed it to the point, the envelope lit up with a clear digital display of English text.

The typeface looked like it had come from an old typewriter. It mentioned a village of women. A small college had been founded in the village, and it had a new Department of Detective Fiction. The department was named after the professor's mother, and it was appropriate that the professor should inaugurate it. The professor was also invited to be a guest at the department for a week. The letter said nothing about the location of the village, or a contact number. It only mentioned a detective who had been invited to deliver the keynote address in the inauguration. It requested the professor to email her acceptance to this detective. Her ticket would be booked as soon as her acceptance was received, and she would travel to the village with the detective, by train.

For Professor 800, it was enough that a department being set up was being named after her mother. She sent her acceptance as soon as she had digested the message. She wrote an email saying that she was available immediately. Very soon, she got an email reply with a ticket attached. The next day, the professor sent brief emails about her programme to the writer and to a journalist friend. She finished packing by the early morning, and by four in the evening she was in a radio taxi headed for New Delhi railway station, armed with an e-ticket.

It was a warm July evening. As usual, the platform was overrun with passengers, coolies and vendors. There was still some time for the train. The professor stood in front of a mobile kiosk adorned with books, magazines and comics, with pulp fiction occupying pride of place.

The professor rested her suitcase on the ground, while she held her handbag close. She browsed the detective novels. It surprised her that the mix of authors had not changed in all these years – Arthur Conan Doyle, Colonel Ranjit, Surendra Mohan Pathak, Gulshan Nanda. She was even more surprised to see her mother's book, *Eight Hundred Miles*. Strangely, though, it did not have her mother's name on the cover. She had read it back in her college days, and she clearly remembered seeing the name in bold red letters. She bought the book, and a cup of steaming milk tea from the next stall, and started reading it as she stood there holding it with one hand.

She had forgotten everything about it. This is how it began: 'Eight hundred miles from Delhi International Airport, there was a village that did not exist in the maps of India.'

The public address system blared an announcement of the train's arrival, interrupting her just as she had savoured this line and a sip of tea. She put the book in her handbag, gulped the tea down, threw the *kullar*, a mud teacup, on to the tracks and manoeuvred herself to the slot for the 'First AC', the first class, air-conditioned, coach. The train stormed into the station and its steel wheels screeched until they came to a grinding halt. The professor imagined a horseman galloping at full speed and then pulling the reins so that his horse whinnied and bucked. The Vice Chancellor's stern visage came to mind, and she shook her head. Reality, not fiction, he had said. Reality, my foot, she thought and she imagined herself leading a cavalry charge into the coach.

When she got to her berth, breathless, she almost fainted. The woman in the black gown and white shoes, the one from the red table at M-800, was waiting for her. Professor 800 seemed to go deaf in the middle of that overwhelming din. The woman's lips were moving. The professor registered the words, 'Welcome, Professor 800. Is it okay to use that name?'

There was a mirror between the seats, and it told her she looked like she had seen a ghost. She nodded, and croaked, 'Thank you.' There was a bottle of water in a holder next to her seat. She steadied her hands, tore off the wrapper and took a draught of water. She brought herself to look the woman in the eye. She saw that this time, the woman had her white hat next to her, on the berth.

'So, you are the detective?' She said. 'Nice hat. Nice shoes.' She smiled. Her voice came out strong now. She felt better.

'Thanks. You can call me Monalika', the woman said.

'Okay', the professor said. 'Nice name, too. It reminds me of Mona Lisa.' She realised she was being quite fatuous, but she couldn't help saying, 'And you are beautiful too.'

'Thanks, but people call me Detective M.', the woman said. 'It's also the name of my company.'

'Oh, that sounds cool.' The professor had completely recovered her poise by now. 'But how do you know my nickname, Professor 800, Detective M. – sounds a bit corny, no?' She gave Detective M. her aggressive-smiley look.

'Oh people know many things about you. After all, you're a famous professor. And don't forget I'm a detective. I always collect details before travelling with someone. It makes the journey fun.'

'Hm, so you know all about me.'

'Of course, I can tell you the colour of your bra.'

'Oh?' the professor smirked. 'Do tell?'

'You're not wearing one', the detective said softly.

The professor gulped. She had thought her loose dress style, and small breasts would not betray her bra-lessness.

'How?'

'That's a secret.' Detective M. leant back with her arms folded.

The professor felt invaded. She remembered the feeling she had got in the lift, of being watched by a hidden camera.

She wanted to go into the offence.

'Okay, tell me one thing. Have you ever visited M-800, the restaurant in Delhi?' She bored into Detective M.'s eyes.

'No, never', the detective said coolly. 'Why ask?'

'Well, I saw someone dressed like you there once.'

'Oh? Like me?' Detective M. raised an eyebrow. 'Maybe she was also a detective.'

'Ha-ha. Maybe.' The professor stood up. 'I'll be back from the washroom.'

When she stepped out of the coach, into the area outside the washroom, she took a deep, long breath. She thought of the writer. She pulled aside the curtain on the window and peered outside. She had to concentrate for some time before she could figure out that it was raining. A few dots of light glimmered in the inky blackness. She suddenly felt very small and helpless as the train hurtled forward with its rhythmic metallic din. She could not get that evening at M-800 out of her mind, and the image of the woman at the red table seemed to get closer each time she tried to blank it out.

She had to struggle to open the washroom door, as usual. It was designed for an iron man. Not that there were too many iron men around. She closed the door behind her with a sense of relief. She looked at herself in the mirror. Her face was still drained of colour. Her hand trembled as she fished out the phone and called the writer. As she poured it all out, she felt the writer's disbelief giving way to concern. She said she would email the detective's photo and also a sound recording, if she could.

The writer told her to stay in touch, and call the police if she continued to feel harassed.

The professor put the phone back, and washed her face thrice with water she cupped in her hands. She felt a little better. She did her hair and touched up her lipstick.

When she went back to the berth, Detective M. seemed to have dozed off. She was resting with her head in the palm of her right hand, with a pillow between her side and upper arm. She did not look ridiculous with those clothes and the hat beside her. If anything, she looked beautiful, mystic, and dangerous. A few strands of black hair had strayed on to her cheek. Her earrings were moonlike and silvery, about the size of ten rupee coins. An earphone lead cut across one of the earrings and got lost in the folds of her attractive top. When she looked closer, the professor made out that her top had a pattern of black fish set against a white background. The fish seemed to move when she looked at them. She shook her head and took a deep breath to steady herself. There was something about the woman's shoes that changed her aura from beautiful to mysterious. The professor looked at the white hat. She thought back to the blue box on the red table in the restaurant.

Detective M. opened her eyes and looked straight at her without blinking. The professor flinched at the steeliness of her gaze.

Detective M. pulled the earphone out of her ear.

'Sorry, I dozed off listening to the music.'

The professor forced the image of the blue box out of her mind and met the detectives' gaze.

'So, you're much into music?' She said.

'Mad for it. You?'

'Me too.'

Detective M. sat up and rested her back against the panel.

'Tell me your favourite song. I'll play it for you.'

'Hm. Mine is … yah, the Amitabh Bacchan-Zeenat Aman song, *Do lafzon ki hai*. But play yours first.'

'Okay, but yours is really nice. Mine is the Dharmendra-Rakhi song from Blackmail – *Pal pal dil ke paas*.' The detective picked up her phone, and the sound filled up the coupe. She played *Do lafzon ki hai* next, and then the theme from *Titanic*. The professor did not offer her comment on the choice, but asked for Rachmaninoff's symphony no. 2 next. The joint playlists continued until the Train Ticket Examiner, the TT, knocked. He asked about the two empty berths in the coupe, and it only took one smile from Detective M to convince him not to release them for other passengers. Dinner was served as soon as the TT left.

'Do you feel like a drink? I have a good vodka', Detective M. said.

'Why not?' The professor smiled.

The train stopped for a while at a small station and picked up speed after the stop. It was still raining outside. The mild buzz of the Absolut lubricated their conversation. Detective M. had much to say about her cases, Professor 800 about her mother's books.

As they talked, Professor 800 got the feeling that Detective M.'s mysterious eyes had a new kind of gleam in them, a promise of danger. The roaring and rocking of the train, the hurtling blobs of light outside the window, the dimness of the light inside – Professor 800 found the atmosphere oppressive. She looked around for a switch, and switched on the main light.

Detective M. looked at her watch. The professor saw that it was two at night. The detective pulled out a yellow safe from below her seat. When she opened it after turning a combination lock in a fluid motion, the professor's heart skipped a beat. Out came the blue box that she had seen in the restaurant. And with it, a pistol. Before the professor's dulled reflex could even suggest a move, the detective had pressed a button on the blue box and pointed the pistol at her nose.

'Don't move. Look there's a silencer', the detective said. 'Not a sound. No movement. It'll take less than a second to finish you off.'

She had just finished speaking when two masked women stormed in. One tied Professor 800's hands, and the other taped up her mouth. Detective M. pulled the stop chain. It had all happened in a few minutes, like the flicking by of a small station in the window. By the time the train slowed down, the two masked women had opened the emergency window. They gathered the professor's items, and as soon as the train shuddered to a halt, they jumped out of the window, bundling the professor along with them. The professor's knees and ribs jarred as she landed on the stony ground. She registered Detective M. pressing another button on the blue box, and within seconds the headlights of a car pierced the dark and the drizzle. The car was a gleaming black Ambassador. The next thing she knew, the professor was in the back seat, between the two masked women. The headlight beams told her that they were on a muddy road with dense jungle on both sides.

The last lines of the story, which were figments of my imagination, seemed to echo in the packed auditorium even after I had finished reading them. The questions that followed were predictable. What happened next? I had no answers. How could I? I was an ordinary writer. Even the professor's writer friend, and the Vice Chancellor, did not have the answers. I signed off saying that only Professor 800 knew.

There is a story behind how I got this story. As it happened, I travelled the same train, in the same coach as the professor. I was all alone. To kill time, I had bought a novel from the bookstall on the platform. It was called *Eight Hundred Miles*. The title was grey on a yellow cover. The writer's name was not printed anywhere on the book.

The first line got me hooked, but the TT walked in before I could move on to the second line. After checking my ticket, the TT asked for my book and flicked through it.

'What do you do?' He asked.

'I write. Fiction.' I said.

'And where did you get this?'

'On the platform.'

I tried to read the TT's face. He seemed to want to share a secret, to unburden himself. As he planted himself on the opposite seat, his belly popped out. Tracing his finger over his mostly white moustache, he said,

'I have a story that you haven't heard before. It happened here, in this coach A1, and it has to do with this novel.' He yawned. 'Today is my last day on the job. I have lost a lot of sleep over this story in the last month. I want to get it out of my head now. So, do you want to hear it?'

The story was long, very long, and the TT sweated, in spite of the chilly air condition, as he told it. There was something about it that made it more than your average story, and I found myself growing intrigued, even a little scared. I looked at the emergency window. It had been repainted, and the red paint was still fresh.

I said, 'I can buy what happened in the coach. But how do you know the rest?'

'From this', he said, and he took out a pink pen drive from his battered old black handbag. 'The rest is in this. I don't know if the professor left it in the bathroom by chance or by design.'

I asked if he had reported all this to the police, and he said he had not.

'Why not?' I asked him. 'Don't you think you could face action if it comes out later?'

'I could. But when I read the story in the pen drive, it was already some time after the incident. I did realise how serious it was, but I thought it was too late to do anything useful.'

'It's nothing to do with the pen drive', I said. 'You should have reported the disappearance as soon as it happened. You've been very lax.'

'Look, I am an old man. Like I said, today is my last day on the job. Had I made a police case out of it, I would have been a key witness. I would have spent the rest of my life trudging the courts. I would have received threats; who knows, they might have killed me. I would rather spend my last days surrounded by the flowers in my lawn, and my grandchildren. Not battling death threats.'

'Do you even know what you are saying?' I asked the man. 'Look'. I shoved the newspaper, with its depressing headlines, under his nose.

In Madhya Pradesh, four members of a terrorist group had broken out of jail. In Chhatisgarh, a bomb explosion had razed a government office to the ground. In Kashmir, a fresh round of artillery fire had started from across the border. In Rajasthan, the women in a village had beaten the *sarpanch*, the village chief, to death after he raped a woman. Some nurses had disappeared from a hospital in Kolkata. The Intelligence Bureau had issued an alert about a possible bomb blast in one of the four metro cities, in which a woman would be used to carry the bomb.

'And look at this article', I said. 'It explains that in the last month or so, many prominent personalities have disappeared from the city. Scientists, doctors, engineers, designers, filmmakers, economists, politicians. And they are all women. Isn't it possible that Professor 800's death is related?'

The TT looked troubled, and lines of worry creased his forehead.

'I don't want to scare you', I continued. 'It's just a line of thinking. If there is anything to what I'm saying, your role will be super important. I think you should step forward and welcome the opportunity. After all, there is a last day in the service of your employer, but there is no such thing in the service of society.'

The TT seemed to be nodding his agreement. Although I did not show it, I was happy that I had been able to change his attitude. I looked at my watch. It was about time for my station. I offered the pen drive back to the TT, but to my surprise he blocked me with a palm, and took out an iPhone from his handbag. He said he had found it in the coach on the night of the incident. It was code-protected, but it might well be the professor's. He suggested I keep both the pen drive and the phone, and do whatever was possible in the case. He said he would help me in every way he could.

I was not prepared for all this. I pondered the situation for a while. I convinced myself that if nothing else, I would get a story out of it. I took the phone and pen drive, and exchanged numbers with the TT before leaving.

I slept an uneasy sleep in my flat in Delhi that night. When I read the newspaper the next morning, a story reminded me of Professor 800. A reporter had toured an area of Chhatisgarh where the Naxalite rebels were the law. They had suspended the Indian constitution and installed a regime that they claimed was dedicated to equality. They had declared many aboriginal areas as the fiefs, and had been at war with the police for many years. I did not have anything by way of evidence, but I was tempted to think that the Naxalites had kidnapped Professor 800.

After breakfast and coffee, I started reading Professor 800's diary from the pink pen drive. The diary mentioned her writer friend very often. At a few places, it also mentioned messages she had sent to a journalist friend.

I called a friend of mine who was an IT expert. It took him a great effort and many hours to hack the phone. I started deconstructing the last phase of Professor 800's known life. From her call history, I saw that most of her calls were to the writer friend. I called this friend. It took a short while for her to open up to me, but once she did it was clear that she was very worried for the professor. She told me about their chat on the fateful night. She wanted to see me right away, and she gave me her address and directions. I was with her in an hour.

We discussed the incident in her plush drawing room. I made special mention of a sensitive piece the professor had written about her mother in the diary. Apparently, she still hoped to meet her. I asked the writer why Professor 800 would have been deluded about it. The writer frowned and excused herself. She came back in a few minutes with some newspaper cuttings. Except for one, all of them were unequivocal about her parents' death. There was one exception, which the writer explained had come out a few months after the blast. By that time, though, that newspaper had closed down. We flogged our network, but all we could find was that a student who had served at the newspaper's office now rented the small house in Daryaganj.

The thing about the exceptional article was that it emphasised the lack of any clinching evidence from the blast-affected coach that conclusively pointed to the professor's parents' death. As I read the article, the opening line from *Eight Hundred Miles* came to my mind for some reason. I kept the thought to myself. I asked the writer about the digital envelope and the detective in the professor's diary. I said that the envelope was most unusual, and should be a good clue. Could we search Professor 800's flat for it?

'Maybe, maybe not', the writer said. 'I mean, we may not find it. She may have taken the envelope with her. I have a key to her flat, though. She was … is, my close friend. We can try if you like.'

We were at her flat as soon as my car could take us there through to Delhi traffic. I was right. The envelope was lying on the dining table. It had a tiny seal, perhaps that of a courier company. We took turns to try to decipher it, but we could not make any more progress than Professor 800 had made. I told the writer that this was the code that would get us to the professor.

I noticed that the writer was not too enthusiastic about my approach. She had a different hypothesis. She said the professor had lived in a fantasy world. She would imagine things that had never been part of her life. She hesitated a little, but then she seemed to make up her mind to talk freely. She said that the detective with the outlandish dress, and the blue box, were almost certainly fictional. I smiled and told her about my discussion with the TT. He had told me that he had seen the detective.

'And we do have this digital envelope in front of us', I said.

The writer looked glum.

'So, the detective existed. Then it's true she was following the professor for some time. You know, the professor also told me about the detective when she called from the train. She even said something about sending me a recording of her conversation with the detective. When I never got a recording, I concluded that she had imagined it. Shall we check her phone for an audio file?'

'Good idea', I said. I looked in the phone, and sure enough, there was an audio file from the day of the professor's disappearance. I played it and we heard it out with rapt attention. We were quiet for a while after it had played out. There was no doubt that a trap had been laid for the professor, and her penchant for the mysterious and her love for her mother had been exploited to the hilt. The question was: who was behind this? The Naxalites? Terrorists? Some unknown extremist group? Or had the professor enacted a life story to efface herself? In any case, I was so enmeshed in this story that there was no going back for me. I asked the writer if I could keep the envelope.

'It's an important link in the plot. Don't you think I should take it to the police?' She said.

I could not fault her logic. I said that she was right, and that I could just keep photos of it. I clicked snaps with my phone, and we left the flat. The writer suggested we talk to the Vice Chancellor. We figured that the case would be more high-profile, and the enquiry more focused, if the First Information Report, FIR, was filed by the University.

The Vice Chancellor spoke to us with lowered, grim eyes. He was sorry that he had compelled the professor to go on leave. He told us he would do everything in his power to trace her. He directed us to the legal cell of the University, and from the response we got, he had probably put in a word with them. We described the case down to the last detail, and the FIR was lodged the next day, and the police started work. Professor 800's vanishing became breaking news on the media. Pretty much every channel covered the story with their own take. This was not an item for a day. It had the potential to take on dimensions that had national and international importance. Professor 800 herself might have felt repulsed at the effects and the treatment that some channels gave the story, but the writer and I were okay with all the noise.

I scanned the channels and papers for three days, and devoured every bit about the case. As the media had already reported on the disappearance of some high-profile women, the professor's case could be viewed as another related episode. Some journalists employed the angle that she had been kidnapped by a terrorist organisation. Other outlets narrowed it down to Naxalites, while a few talked about Professor 800's emotional troubles with her parents' death. There were comments on the rising insecurity in trains. I thought that the analyses were not complete and factual. The police had a single official statement and they steadfastly stuck to it: their teams were completely dedicated to the investigation and all leads were being explored. I knew the real story: the police reserved their dedication for politicians and industrialists, while the crime graph in the city continued to rise.

I had never met Professor 800, nor had I heard much about her before she disappeared. But the TT's story had sucked me in and now, it refused to let go. I had often wondered if my buying that novel, and then boarding that very coach of the same train, was really a coincidence. Or had I been trapped like the professor? I had read many books about hypnotism. One night, I woke up in a cold sweat, wondering if all this was the result of a hypnotic spell – why else had I let the case possess me? That morning, I started checking out the professor's life thoroughly and unbiased, as if starting from scratch.

I researched her books first, and each of them gave me a sense of deja vu. One of the books was about Marquez's *One Hundred Years of Solitude*. It made me a complete fan of Professor 800. Her critique and her style were extraordinary. An essay on Woody Allen's story *The Kugelmass Episode* took me to an alternate world, one in which the line between fantasy and reality melted away. Where the University and its Vice Chancellor found signs of mental illness, I saw nothing but the height of literary prowess. True, not everyone could look at the world through the professor's lenses. I knew the world needed more professors like her, not less.

I never figured what possessed me to decide I could not leave the case to the loud reporters, and to buy a Honda Shine motorbike, put *Eight Hundred Miles* and some other effects in my bag, and set off on National Highway 8, towards Delhi Airport. I chose to go towards the old terminal, the one which housed the international airport when the book was written. I figured from the map that there were three directions one could take from there, and therefore

I would have to travel eight hundred miles on each of them in the worst case.

For fifteen days, I drove the potholed, grimy roads of my part of the country. I became a wanderer, an itinerant. I felt dust and soot oozing out of my ears. My butt felt the throb of the bike long hours after I had got off it. There was no trace of the courier company that might have sent that envelope. I decided to turn back towards Delhi. I had finished a lunch of *parathas* and *daal* at a *dhaab*a, a roadside eating joint, and driven for two hours, when the sky turned dark with clouds that looked about ready to burst. I stopped, put on a yellow raincoat and revved until my wrists hurt so that I could get to a small hamlet two kilometres down the road.

I made it into the village just as the first drops of rain pelted the visor of my helmet. A shopkeeper told me that there were courier companies in the village. I did not have high hopes, but I went to each of them in turn.

I found success at the third one. The man at the makeshift desk was prepared to take my envelope, and – for an extra charge – deliver it so the recipient would never know who the sender was.

I said I needed a photo of the sealed envelope. The man refused at first, but some more money – without a receipt this time – helped him change his mind. The guy had a sad look as he took the money, and I was tempted to ask if he always wore that look. I did not. I matched the photo in my camera with the one he showed me. It was a match, as far as I could make out. At least the string of Xs, Ys, Zs and 0s seemed to be almost the same.

A sense of peace came over me. My tiredness vanished. I felt light as I stepped out of that small, dusty office. It was still raining, but I did not care. Pretty soon – it felt like no time at all – I had scanned that whole town. A muddy river ran on the other side of it. In the distance, beyond the river, I made out railway tracks. On the far side of the tracks, there was dense jungle. I drove past a ramshackle bridge in the pouring rain. A decrepit railway crossing then led me past the railway line, and from there a road of sorts went into the jungle.

I stopped just before the jungle. I flipped the visor and let the rain pour on my closed eyes and face. It was a gentle rain, and my eyes loved the soft massage. I took a deep breath and smelt the freshness of the jungle. It was dark by then. Only a couple of lights glimmered in the distance through the warm rain. There was no sign of any man or woman. One of the lights marked the presence of a hut. I drove up to it. It was open on one side, and it had a bench. I rode my motorbike into the hut, and removed my raincoat. I wiped the streams of water off my hair and face, dried my hands on my hips, and gingerly picked up the worn-out *Eight Hundred Miles* from my bag, taking care not to wet it.

I started reading it in the faint light. After a while, I flipped back to the opening that had haunted me all these days. This time, the third line resonated with new meaning. It was the same as the beginning of the text in the envelope that Professor 800 had received. I looked at the photo in my phone again. Yes, there it was. A small community of women, with a small college in which a new department of Detective Fiction was being established.

The roar of a train came closer and then receded into the background. It was still raining. I looked at the railway track gleaming in the distance, and then at the mud track heading into the jungle from the hut. The air had changed now. It had become more still. I thought I saw a black Ambassador lurch to a stop near my motorbike. It got there without a sound. I heard the loud click of its rear left door opening. A pair of gleaming white shoes emerged. The woman in those shoes stood tall as she stepped out. I saw her white hat tilted forward, covering her face, and next I saw her press a button on a blue box with a slender thumb. I felt faint. I realised my book had fallen to the ground. Its first line came to my mind again: 'Eight hundred miles from Delhi International Airport, there was a village that did not exist in the maps of India.'

Author Biographies

Bhalchandra JOSHI was born in 1956. He is an engineer by profession, but he also has an MA degree in English literature. He started writing fiction in the late 1980s. He has worked on the folk arts and tales of the Nimar region of south-west Madhya Pradesh state. He edited the magazine *Yatharth* for some time, and was the editor of the 'New Writing' issue of *Kathadesh* in 2012. He has authored scripts for Indian TV serials, and translated stories between Indian languages and also into English and French. He has published six collections of short stories, a textbook on disaster management and a work of literary criticism. His works have won him six awards.

Dileep SHAKYA was born in 1976 in Joura, Madhya Pradesh. He obtained a BA in psychology from IEHE Bhopal and a Ph.D. in modern literature from Jahawarlal Nehru University. He became Assistant Professor of Hindi Literature at Jamia Millia Islamia University, New Delhi, in 2002, and is presently Visiting Professor at the University of Budapest, Hungary. Dileep Shakya is known as a poet and fiction writer, and has made a rmark in the field of cinema writing and poetry criticism. His poetry collection published in 2015 by Bhartiya Jnanpith, New Delhi, has won the tenth Navlekhan Award. His publications also include three books of poetry criticism, a 'diary fiction' series on the Chambal region serialised in *Pakhi magazine*; a cinema-writing column in *Yudhrat Aam Aadmi magazine* since March 2014, and short stories in *Kathadesh*. He is currently working on translations from Hungarian literature.

Nivedita JENA, born in 1974, is an officer with Union Bank of India. She has been an active writer, theatre actor and playwright in Odia, the language of Orissa. She is currently conducting research in Odia children's theatre. As a social activist, she conducts theatre workshops for disadvantaged children. Nivedita Jena has authored three collections of Odia plays, an Odia short story collection titled *Aalo*

Sakhi, and an Odia analytical work titled *Tikinatua*. She has had 45 Odia, and 8 Hindi essays published in various magazines. She received several prizes, including an award from the Sahitya Akademi, the Indian national academy of literature, for her play *Haat Aur Chaitu*.

Pratibhu BANERJEE was born in 1963 in Pendra, Chattisgarh. He graduated in science and specialised in Hindi literature at the postgraduate level. He holds a banking certification from the Indian Institute of Banking and Finance and is currently a senior faculty member at the Staff Training Centre of the Union Bank of India in Bhubaneshwar, Orissa. He has authored *Bulbul, Why Don't You Fly*, a collection of short stories, *Tapan the Circuswallah*, a young adult novel, a primary guide to Amarkantak, and non-fiction books on banking and rural development. He has had stories published in several literary magazines, and has worked with Akashvani, the Indian national radio broadcasting service. He has won awards from his writing for his short story collection, for a short story titled *Mother, when will Munu Come?* and for an essay titled *I, Chattisgarh*.

Premchand GANDHI was born in 1967 in Jaipur, Rajasthan. He holds B.Com. and MA Hindi degrees from Rajasthan University. His first story was published in 1984 in a college magazine. Since then, he has had poems, stories, surveys, essays and translations published in many newspapers and magazines. He has been a culture journalist and a regular columnist. He has won the Laxman Prasad Mandloi and Rajendra Bohra Awards for poetry, the Pandit Gokul Chandra Rao Award for cultural writing, and has a prize from Jawahar Kala Kendra for theatre. His theatrical retelling of the story of the *Ramayana* from a feminist viewpoint, *Sita Lila*, has been widely staged and acclaimed.

Vandana SHUKLA was born in Gwalior, Madhya Pradesh. She holds a B.Ed. and Master degrees in Hindi Literature and Hindustani classical music. She has been a theatre and music artist and presenter with Akashvani, the Indian public radio broadcasting service. She has written and directed plays based on three of Premchand's stories. Her first story was published in the Hindi literary magazine *Vagarth* in 2010, and by now she has publications to her credit in most well-known Hindi literary magazines. Vandana Shukla has published a novel and a short story collection, and has another short story collection, *Doosri Ibaarat* (A Second Writing), forthcoming. Her poems are included in the curriculum of the Indology department at Croatia University, and her stories have been translated into Chinese and English. Her awards include the Kamleshwar Memorial Award from *Kathabimb* magazine, and awards from *Kadambari* magazine and BSF India.

Vivek MISHRA was born in 1970 in Jhansi, Uttar Pradesh. He graduated in science with a specialisation in dental health and did his postgraduate studies in journalism and mass communication. His first novel *Dominic Ki Wapasi* (Dominic's Return) won an award from the publisher Kitabghar Publications. He has three short story collections to his credit, and some of his stories are included in graduate curricula. His stories have been translated into Bengali, and a collection of poetry, *Light Through a Labyrinth*, has been translated into English and published by Writer's Workshop, Kolkata. He won the 2015 Yashpal Prize from the Uttar Pradhesh Hindi Sansthan.